"Did you hear that?" Sam asked Emma as they came off stage.

"The choreographer really thought I was good!"

"Well, of course she did!" Emma said. "I just wonder if I looked like a fool."

"You were fabulous," Sam told her loyally. "Hey, look who just hit the stage."

Diana and Lorell were both in the next threesome. The music started up and they began dancing.

"Oh, my God, she's great," Sam whispered, her heart sinking. "I will die if she gets to dance with me!"

"They wouldn't really ever hire Diana, would they?" Emma asked.

"Not if I have anything to say about it," Sam muttered. She looked over at Pres as he watched the dancers intently from across the room. "Excuse me while I go use my considerable influence," she said, and headed straight for him.

The SUNSET ISLAND series
by Cherie Bennett

Sunset Island
Sunset Kiss
Sunset Dreams
Sunset Farewell
Sunset Reunion
Sunset Secrets
Sunset Heat
Sunset Promises
Sunset Scandal
Sunset Whispers

Sunset Whispers

CHERIE BENNETT

SPLASH™

A BERKLEY / SPLASH BOOK

SUNSET WHISPERS is an original publication of The Berkley Publishing Group. This work has never appeared before in book form.

SUNSET WHISPERS

A Berkley Book / published by arrangement with General Licensing Company, Inc.

PRINTING HISTORY
Berkley edition / September 1992

A GLC BOOK

Splash is a trademark belonging to General Licensing Company, Inc.

ISBN: 0-425-13386-9

A BERKLEY BOOK ® TM 757,375
Berkley Books are published by The Berkley Publishing Group, 200 Madison Avenue, New York, New York 10016.
The name "BERKLEY" and the "B" logo are trademarks belonging to Berkley Publishing Corporation.

PRINTED IN THE UNITED STATES OF AMERICA

10 9 8 7 6 5 4 3 2

This book is for Jeff

ONE

"I can see it now," Samantha Bridges said, staring dreamily toward the ocean, "me, at the MTV awards, winning big. I walk up to the stage in my drop-dead dress slit up to heaven, and thank all the little people . . ."

"Yo, earth to Sam," Carrie Alden called, interrupting Sam's reverie. "You're auditioning to be a backup singer, not a major recording artist."

"And I believe 'audition' is the operative word there," Emma Cresswell added. "As in you don't have the job yet."

"You two definitely think too small," Sam said, reaching into her beach bag for a bottle of sunscreen. "First of all, you guys know I'm going to get the gig. And second of all, today's backup singer could be tomorrow's star."

Sam spread a layer of sunscreen on her long legs. She and her two best friends, Emma and Carrie, were spending their morning lolling on the beach. Although Sam's summer job was to take care of Allie and Becky Jacobs, precocious fourteen-year-old twins (who insisted they didn't need any "care," thank you very much), they had gone fishing with their dad, so she had the day free.

"Hey, look at this," Carrie said, sitting up. "There's an ad in the *Breakers* for the auditions."

Sam stuck her neck over Carrie's shoulder to look at the ad.

FLIRTING WITH DANGER, TOP REGIONAL ROCK BAND, SEEKS THREE BACKUP SINGER/DANCERS FOR LOCAL AND TOURING GIGS.

The ad went on to give the time and place of the auditions.

"Oh, just great," Sam moaned. "Now there'll be a zillion girls there."

"You can handle the competition," Carrie assured her.

"Right," Emma agreed. "How many of them will have danced professionally like you have?"

"True," Sam agreed, contemplatively winding a lock of her long red hair around her finger. She had, after all, been a professional dancer at Disney World—before she was fired for being too original, that is. And she *was* dating the bass player from Flirting with Danger—or the Flirts, as everyone called them. Surely she had a leg up on the competition!

"Hey, listen," Sam said, flopping over onto her stomach. "I've got an idea. I think you guys should audition with me."

"No way!" Carrie said, laughing.

"Way!" Sam said, nudging Carrie in the leg.

"Hey, I'm strictly a behind-the-scenes type," Carrie said.

"But you're Billy's girlfriend," Sam pointed out, naming the very hunky lead singer of the Flirts. "If anybody is a shoe-in, it's you."

"Even if I *were* going to audition, which I'm not," Carrie began, "Billy wouldn't choose me just because I'm his girlfriend."

Sam's raised her eyebrows skeptically.

"You sure don't know guys very well, girl-friend," Sam said. "They don't do all their thinking with their *heads*, if you catch my drift."

"Well, neither do you!" Emma pointed out with a laugh.

Shielding the sun from her eyes with her hand, Sam turned to Emma. "How about you, Em? Want to audition with me?"

"Oh, I don't think so—" Emma began.

"Come on, it'll be fun!" Sam urged her. "Just think how good your virginal blond ice-maiden look would be next to wild red-headed Amazon me!"

"I admit it sounds like fun," Emma said in a small voice, "but—"

"No 'buts'!" Sam crowed. "Oh, please do it with me, Emma. Please, please. It would be a total blast!"

"I don't really think they'd ever pick me," Emma said.

"Just do the audition with me, then," Sam begged.

Emma cocked her head to one side contemplatively. "Okay," she said finally. "I will."

"Well, get down, Emma!" Sam exclaimed, hugging her. "I'm totally psyched!"

4

Sam turned over on her towel to sun her back. She was so glad Emma was going to audition with her. Having one of her best friends go through it with her would make it less scary. The truth of the matter was, no matter how confident she acted, she was really nervous about the audition. *Everyone expects me to get picked*, Sam said to herself, *but what if I don't? It will be totally humiliating*.

She never thought she'd have a prayer talking either one of her friends into auditioning with her. Carrie was an intellectual who preferred taking photos to posing for them, and Emma was a rich heiress who could buy her own record label if she chose to, though she never flaunted her wealth. Sam was the one who longed for the spotlight, and dreamed of being featured on *Lifestyles of the Rich and Famous*.

"Now, this is what I call one beautiful sight," came a sexy southern voice from above them. Sam turned over to see Pres admiring the three of them through a pair of dark sunglasses. She took in his acid green surfer jams that showed off his dark, golden tan and sinewy muscles to perfection.

"Right back at ya!" Sam said, sitting up

and smiling. "Is this a coincidence or were you out hunting for me?"

"Both," Pres said with a lazy grin. He dropped to the sand next to Sam. "I went by the Jacobses' to see you, but no one was home, so I thought I'd come for a swim. And dang if I didn't run into you anyway."

"Yeah, dang," Sam agreed. She loved teasing Pres about his accent and his colorful expressions. They were a far cry from the way people talked in Maine or in her home state of Kansas.

"Anybody for a swim?" Carrie asked, throwing a pointed look at Emma.

Emma stood up and brushed the sand from her legs. "I can take a hint," Emma said good-naturedly. She and Carrie ran toward the ocean.

"You look good enough to eat," Pres murmured, leaning toward Sam and kissing her lightly.

Sam looked down at her new neon pink and white polka-dotted bikini. "You wouldn't think so little material would cost so much money," she said with a shrug.

"Well, in that case," Pres said, "I believe I'll have seconds." He kissed Sam again.

This time Sam kissed him back, a long delicious kiss.

"Whoa, time out," she called, coming up for air.

Pres laughed and rubbed his hand across a two-day growth of beard. "Believe it or not, I was lookin' for you for reasons other than your luscious lips," he said. He pulled a white paper out of the back pocket of his jams. "I brought you the application form for the F.F.A."

Sam's fingers were shaking as she took the paper from him. Pres had told her all about the F.F.A.—the Family Finders Agency. It was a national nonprofit group that helped people who had been adopted find their birth parents.

Sam had discovered only that summer that she was adopted. She'd been devastated by the news. She just couldn't understand how her parents could have kept her identity a secret from her for her entire life. True, she'd always felt different from them and her younger sister, Ruth Ann, and she didn't look like any of them, but *adopted?*

She still wouldn't know the truth if she hadn't needed her birth certificate for a job offer dancing overseas. Her parents had still been keeping the truth from her but she'd inadvertently discovered their secret.

Sam had been thrown into a terrible turmoil. Sure, she didn't always get along with her parents or agree with the way they looked at the world—they were perfectly happy in the hick little town of Junction, Kansas—but she'd always trusted them. Now she felt that if they could lie to her about this, they could lie to her about anything.

For a while she'd been so angry she wouldn't even speak to them. Now they were talking again, but Sam felt a coldness there that she couldn't seem to get over.

Pres had really helped her in dealing with the situation, though. She had been surprised to find out that he was adopted, too. He'd known his whole life, and seemed to have a great perspective on it.

"Thanks," Sam said to Pres in a low voice. "This could change my entire life."

"Just take it slow," Pres advised. "I've heard they've been looking for some people's parents for years and years and haven't come up with squat. There aren't any guarantees."

"But you said that sometimes they find birth parents right away," Sam said. "That might happen to me."

"It might," Pres allowed. "But it also might not."

"I'm going to fill this out this afternoon," Sam said with shining eyes. She wasn't going to allow Pres's warnings to dampen her excitement. She put the application in her beach bag, then leaned over to kiss Pres lightly. "Thanks," she said softly. "I really appreciate it."

"Shucks, weren't nothin', ma'am," Pres teased.

"Hey, I saw your ad for the backup auditions in the *Breakers*," Sam said, digging her toes in the sand. "You're going to get a ton of girls now that you're advertising."

"That's the whole point, sweet meat," Pres said with a grin. "There's an ad in the Portland *Press-Herald*, too."

"Oh, great," Sam moaned. "You'll get ten tons of girls."

"Nice image," Pres said.

Sam swatted his arm. "Just remember, I expect to be treated like a diamond among the cubic zirconia," she warned him.

"Hey, we'll judge everybody fairly," Pres said.

Sam leaned close to him. "Meaning I have no influence with the judges?" she asked in a low voice.

Pres laughed. "You are too much, girl. You're a great dancer, so you don't have to worry too much about 'influence.'"

"True," Sam agreed blithely.

Inside, though, she didn't feel nearly so secure. It wasn't her dancing she was worried about, it was her singing. She definitely was not the world's greatest singer. Pres had been dazzled by her dancing in the past, but he'd never heard her sing. *I'll practice in the shower every day between now and the audition,* Sam vowed to herself.

Pres glanced at his sport watch. "I gotta motor. I'm working on a new tune this afternoon with Billy."

"Feel free to dedicate it to me," Sam said innocently.

Although she'd never admit it, it rankled her a bit that Billy had written a song for Carrie, and Pres hadn't followed suit for her. But then, she and Pres weren't nearly as serious as Carrie and Billy, she reminded herself. Not yet, anyway.

10

"Well, I guess I could," Pres reflected, stroking his chin. "It's called 'She Done Me Wrong.'"

"On second thought, I can wait," Sam said sweetly. "Thanks again for the application."

"No problem," Pres answered. "I'll call you."

Sam watched Pres walk away, then she pulled the application from her bag and scanned it. She could hardly wait to send it in.

This, she said to herself, *just might change my life*.

TWO

"You make me totally sick, Allie!" Becky screamed from down the hall. "I hate your guts!"

"It's not my fault if Jake thinks you're a pig!" Allie screamed back. "Lose some weight!"

"I weigh exactly the same as you, lard ass!" Becky yelled.

"You do not. I lost five pounds and you know it!" Allie screamed back.

Sam sighed deeply and padded across her room to shut the door, hoping to block out the sound of the twins' arguing. They had returned from their fishing trip in a foul mood, and as usual, their latest fight had to do with a guy.

Very cute and almost totally identical-looking—except that Allie had cut her hair earlier in the summer—they were also terribly insecure. They seemed to need constant reinforcement from the opposite sex that they were cute. Sam figured it had something to do with their mom running out on them, but the whole thing was too complex for her to sort out. Their father wasn't a big help, either. He couldn't really communicate with the girls, and lately he erred on the side of being too lenient for their own good.

"I'm never eating anything again!" Sam heard Becky sob as she shut the door.

Oh, great, Sam said to herself. *Now I'm going to have to try to force-feed her.*

She lay back down on her bed and picked up her pen. She'd filled out as much of the Family Finders application as she could. The little she knew of her past came from her birth certificate. Her parents hadn't told her much else. The subject seemed to make them extremely uncomfortable.

Well, I hope that's enough, Sam said to herself, signing the bottom. She put the application into an envelope and addressed it, then stuck a stamp on it. First thing in the morning she'd mail it off to the branch office in Bangor.

"Hey, Sam, can I come in?" one of the twins asked, pounding on Sam's door.

"Sure," Sam said. She didn't really want to deal with either Becky or Allie at that particular moment, but she couldn't very well say no. They were her job.

"Did you see this?" Becky asked, entering the room and thrusting a copy of the *Breakers* at Sam.

Becky had the newspaper opened to the ad for backup singer/dancers for the Flirts.

"Sure I saw it," Sam said.

"I want to audition," Becky said, sitting on Sam's bed.

"Oh, sure, they'd really hire a tub like you," Allie snorted from the doorway.

"What is it with you two tonight?" Sam asked them.

"There was this really cute guy on the fishing boat," Allie said, "and he liked me better than Becky, so she's pissed."

"He didn't like you better," Becky said. "You just threw yourself at him."

"Yeah, well, he couldn't even have gotten his arms around you!" Allie shot back.

"Oh, yeah? Well—" Becky began.

"Hey, time out!" Sam yelled. "This is

ridiculous. Neither of you is the least bit fat."

"I'm five pounds thinner," Allie pointed out smugly.

"Fine," Sam said, rolling her eyes. Allie had recently embarked on a starvation diet that Sam was having little luck talking her out of.

"I'm going to lose ten," Becky said.

"You guys do not need to lose any weight," Sam said firmly.

Becky's eyes narrowed. "I bet you're just saying that so we won't look good enough to get picked as backup singers for the Flirts, and you will."

"Yeah," Allie agreed. "You don't want the competition."

"This is a dumb conversation," Sam said. "You two are not auditioning for the Flirts."

"Yes, we are," Becky said.

"No, you're not," Sam corrected her. "You're too young."

"I don't see any age restrictions in this ad," Becky said.

"That's because there aren't any," Allie pointed out.

"Look, it might not say there are any,"

Sam began, "but the Flirts are not interested in fourteen-year-old backup singers."

"How do you know?" Becky asked coolly.

"Yeah," Allie agreed. "We don't look fourteen, and we're very mature."

Oh, sure, Sam thought to herself, *a minute ago they were ready to kill each other, and now it's them against the world.*

"Sorry, guys, I know what I'm talking about," Sam said.

"Hey, anyone for ice cream?" Mr. Jacobs called from downstairs.

"Do we have butter pecan?" Becky yelled to her dad.

"Sure do!" he called back.

"I thought you weren't ever eating anything again," Allie said to her sister.

"No one starts a diet at night, stupid," Becky said, getting up to go downstairs. "I'll start in the morning."

The two girls left the room. Sam could hear them bickering their way down the hall, and she shook her head ruefully. She and Ruth Ann might have nothing in common, but at least they didn't fight like Becky and Allie did.

"Hey, Sam!" one of the twins called upstairs. "Pres is here!"

An unexpected break from the monsters, Sam thought, running her fingers through her curls before she ran downstairs and out the front door.

Pres was leaning against his motorcycle with Allie next to him.

"Want to take me for a ride on your bike?" she was asking Pres. "I'd hold on real tight," she added.

"Sorry, sugar, another time," Pres said easily.

"Hi there," Sam said. "What's up?"

"Billy and I finished writing that tune," Pres told her. "I think it might just be killer."

"That's great," Sam said.

"How's about a celebratory bike ride?" Pres asked her. "It looks like we're gonna have a hellified sunset."

"Why are you going to take her out on the bike and not me?" Allie asked, her hands on her hips.

"Allie, you are being really obnoxious," Sam said. "Why don't you go have some ice cream inside."

"I don't eat ice cream," Allie answered coolly.

"Lately you don't eat at all," Sam muttered under her breath.

"I heard that," Allie said. "Do you know there is a whole group of people who believe you can live on air?"

"Air?" Pres repeated.

"Yes," Allie said. "Only pigs like Becky need to eat food, especially ice cream."

Sam rolled her eyes. "Allie, please tell your dad I'll be back in a little while," she said, climbing on the back of Pres's bike.

"Maybe I will and maybe I won't," Allie said, turning on her heel and heading into the house.

"That is one unhappy child," Pres said, handing Sam a helmet.

"I know," Sam sighed. "I vacillate between wanting to hug her and wanting to kill her."

Pres started up the bike, and Sam wrapped her arms around his hard, muscled waist. They zoomed down the street, and headed for the quiet of the dunes. Sam closed her eyes and let the feeling of the wind in her face take over her senses. *If only life were as simple as riding on this bike*, she thought.

When they arrived at the dunes, the sun

was just setting, putting on a richly-hued show in the sky. Sam and Pres dropped down to the sand and gazed at the horizon.

"Sometimes I think there's no art we mortal types can make to equal God's," Pres murmured.

"But Pres," Sam said with a mischievous look, "those pretty colors come from pollution filtered through the sun's rays."

Pres gave her an arched stare. "Girl, you haven't got a romantic bone in your body."

"Hey, I have lots of romantic bones in my body," Sam said.

"Really?" Pres asked. "This one?" He tickled her in the ribs. "Or maybe this one?" He tickled her on the other side.

"Stop!" Sam shrieked with laughter as his fingers pressed into her playfully. She kicked hard and managed to roll him over in the sand, pinning him down. "Aha!" she crowed triumphantly, her hands holding his wrists down as hard as she could.

"You don't think I'd really struggle out from under here, do you?" he asked her.

"I guess not," she said with a smile.

"You guess right," he answered.

Sam leaned over and kissed him. Her

hands dropped from his wrists and he wrapped his arms around her.

"We're missing the sunset," Sam informed him.

"What sunset?" Pres asked in a low voice, pulling Sam down for another kiss.

"Well, well, as I live and breathe," a nasty female voice trilled near Sam's ear. "You never know what sort of trash you'll find when you take a walk on the beach."

Sam rolled off Pres and looked up into the smug face of Lorell Courtland who was accompanied by her friend Diana De Witt. Lorell and Diana were probably the two most hateful girls Sam had ever encountered in her life. They seemed to live to make Sam, Emma, and Carrie miserable.

"Sam, I realize that back where you come from girls do it any old place," Diana said, "but here where it's civilized we like to use a bed."

Sam could feel her cheeks blushing, and it made her angry that she let these two cretins embarrass her.

"Well, I guess you know all about beds, Diana," Sam replied. "Since you've been in one with everybody."

"Not everybody," Diana said sweetly, eyeing Pres pointedly.

Pres laughed and sat up. "Diana, you are one of a kind."

"That's true," Diana agreed. "Try me some time and see."

"Oh, please, excuse me while I throw up," Sam said.

"Funny to run into you like this," Diana said, ignoring Sam completely. "Lorell and I were just talking about the Flirts' ad in the *Breakers* for backup singers. Do you think we should audition?"

"Sure," Pres said easily, "if you feel like it."

"I think it would be fun to be in the Flirts," Diana said, shaking her chestnut curls out of her eyes. "Think how close we'd get."

"Do you two think you could get lost now?" Sam asked. "Try walking straight toward the ocean and keep going."

"Come on, Diana," Lorell said, brushing some sand off her leg. "I believe these two have to finish—what do they call it back in Kansas?—rutting."

Diana laughed along with Lorell and they moseyed on down the beach.

"God, they make me sick," Sam spat out.

"Hey, don't let them get to you," Pres said, putting his arm around her. "They're just fooling."

"How can you take it so casually?" Sam asked, shaking off Pres's arm with annoyance.

"They're not important enough to take seriously," Pres reasoned. "Anyway, they're just looking to get a rise out of you. If you let them get to you, then you let them win."

"You wouldn't really hire either of them as backup singers for the Flirts, would you?" Sam asked.

"I'm only one of the guys doing the picking," Pres reminded her.

"Yeah, but if one of you says no to someone, that person must be out," Sam reasoned. "You guys are too tight to hire a backup singer that one of you hates."

"I suppose that's true," Pres agreed. "But I don't hate those girls."

"Well, you should," Sam snapped. "They treat me like dirt, and you're supposed to care about me."

"I do care about you," Pres said. "But I'm not wasting my energy hating them over this stupid feud ya'll have."

"It's not a stupid feud!" Sam cried. She was really hurt. "This is one-sided bitchiness. No, worse than that, they say and do things that are really hurtful." She was thinking about the time Diana had actually seduced Emma's boyfriend, Kurt Ackerman just to spite Emma. She even suspected Lorell of intentionally setting their dingy adrift at sea during a yacht party.

"Okay, maybe they're hateful," Pres allowed. "But don't let them drag you down to their level."

"You just don't get it," Sam muttered.

"Forget about them," Pres urged her, putting his arm back around her shoulder.

"I have to get back," Sam said tersely, getting up from the sand. The romantic mood she'd been in had been completely destroyed, compliments of Diana and Lorell.

Pres stood up and put his arms around Sam's waist. "Hey, let's kiss and make up."

"We're not fighting," Sam said, but she could hear the petulance in her own voice.

"Good," Pres said, and brought his lips down softly on Sam's.

She gave in to the kiss. It felt too wonderful to hold back.

"Did you fill out the application for the

F.F.A?" he asked her, nuzzling his face in her hair.

"Yeah, I'll mail it in the morning," Sam said.

"Great," Pres murmured. He kissed her neck, her jaw, and the tip of her ear before pressing his mouth against her lips one more time.

This guy is one of the great kissers of all time, she said to herself.

They rode back to the Jacobs home in silence, Sam looking up at the full moon. It felt so good to be pressed up against Pres, watching the stars twinkle in the sky. Still, it bothered her that he didn't understand about Diana and Lorell. He trivialized it, in fact. *If he really cared about me*, Sam asked herself, *wouldn't my fights be his fights?*

But even as she asked herself the question, she already knew the answer.

THREE

"Hey, Allie, how about eating some breakfast?" Sam asked the next morning as she watched Allie sipping at her second cup of black coffee.

"Food is so boring," Allie intoned.

Sam sighed and came to sit next to Allie at the kitchen table. "Remember Daphne Whittinger?" Sam asked. "She was anorexic, you know. Look how sick she got."

Sam thought maybe the mention of Daphne would bang some sense into Allie's stubborn head. Daphne was a terribly insecure girl whose family had a summer home on the island. The summer before, she'd dieted herself to skeletal thinness, then had flipped out completely. After spending a long time in rehab, she'd returned to the island, allegedly cured. But she'd been secretly harboring some horrible fantasy that Emma was responsible for all the troubles in her life, and had actually tried to kill her.

"Daphne Whittinger is totally looney tunes, I'm not," Allie commented.

"I am so hungry," Becky said, bopping into the kitchen. She opened the bread box and took out a large onion roll.

"Why not have three or four?" Allie said nastily.

Becky opened the refrigerator to get out the margarine. "I'm having one, if you don't mind," she said.

"I thought you were starting a diet," Allie said smugly.

"One onion roll is okay . . . isn't it?" Becky asked Sam.

"Of course it is," Sam said.

"How are my girls this morning?" Mr. Jacobs said cheerfully, coming into the kitchen and pouring himself some coffee.

"Just fine," Allie said breezily, sipping at her coffee.

"Would you like me to make some breakfast?" Sam asked Mr. Jacobs.

"Oh, no, I'll just grab a yogurt, then I'm off to the gym." Mr. Jacobs had recently lost a lot of weight, and had started working out.

"I'd like Allie to eat breakfast," Sam said. "She's just drinking black coffee." Sam hated to go to him with problems about the twins—it was almost as if she felt more like one of them than like an adult—but she was really concerned about Allie.

"It's a good idea to eat some breakfast, honey," Mr. Jacobs said to his daughter.

"I lost five pounds," Allie said proudly.

"Did you?" he asked. "Well, good for you. You know there's a tendency toward plumpness in our family."

Becky, whose onion roll was halfway to her mouth, put it down and stared at it.

"So, I'm off," Mr. Jacobs said, taking a yogurt from the refrigerator. "See you later."

"See?" Allie told Sam. "Even Dad approves of what I'm doing. So butt out." She pushed back her chair and ran upstairs.

"Geez," Becky muttered, "this is even worse than her I-want-to-be-a-nun phase."

"Well, if she loses any more weight, I'm going to have a really serious talk with your dad," Sam promised. She grabbed a sponge and swiped it across the counter. Sometimes

29

she couldn't believe how irresponsible Dan Jacobs was.

After Sam convinced Becky that it really was okay to eat the onion roll, she went upstairs and got ready to take the girls to the club. As she hoisted her beach bag onto her shoulder, she picked up the envelope containing her F.F.A. application and dropped it in her bag.

"Those auditions for backup singers are tomorrow, aren't they?" Allie said as she and Becky got into the car.

"Well, they start tomorrow," Sam said, putting the key into the ignition. "Pres said they're expecting a lot of girls, so they're planning to narrow down the field."

"We still want to audition," Becky said.

"We already had this conversation," Sam reminded her. She turned onto Beach Avenue.

"Hey, we don't need your permission to do what we want," Allie said.

"Yeah," Becky agreed. "It's not up to you, it's up to the Flirts."

"Fine," Sam said as she stopped at a red light. "Don't take my word for it. Ask them, so you can really feel like total fools." Sam pulled up to the tiny post office. "Be right back," she told the twins, "I just have to mail something." Sam hopped out of the car and dropped the envelope into the mailbox. Her heart raced a little in anticipation of the exciting process she was starting. That form was going to lead to her finding her real parents.

The twins were quiet as Sam drove to the country club. Sam watched Becky in the rearview mirror nervously biting her nails down to the quick. She sighed. Sometimes she felt like the twins needed professional help. *Someone who knows a hell of a lot more than I do.*

As soon as Sam parked the car, the twins dashed off to meet some friends. Sam made her way to the main pool where she spotted Carrie, Emma, and Kurt.

It's good to see Kurt laughing again, Sam reflected as she walked toward the group. Recently Kurt had been arrested as a suspect in a burglary. He hadn't had an alibi and it had looked so bad that while he was awaiting trial, the club had actually suspended him from his job as swimming instructor.

Emma and his friends had stood by him, though, and with the help of Darcy Laken, a very perceptive girl who Emma had met while collecting for a local charity on the island, helped find the real criminal and clear Kurt's name.

"Well, don't the three of you look like an ad for carefree youth," Sam said, dropping her beach bag next to an empty chaise lounge.

"Sure," Carrie agreed. "Nothing more important than what number sunscreen to use ever enters my head."

"You missed the funniest sight," Emma said. "Katie and Chloe made up a water ballet and put it on in the kiddie pool." Emma was referring to four-year-old Katie Hewitt, whom she took care of, and five-year-old Chloe Templeton, whom Carrie took care of.

"What I wouldn't give to be taking care of little kids instead of the monsters," Sam sighed, stretching out on her chaise. "Allie is on a no-eating kick, and her father encourages her when she says she's losing weight."

Kurt frowned. "Those girls do *not* need to lose weight."

"Try telling them that," Sam sighed.

Kurt gave Emma a kiss. "Right now I have to go teach a diving lesson," he said. "But if I see the twins I'll make some comment about how they don't need to lose an ounce or something."

"Good luck," Sam called to Kurt. He waved as he walked toward the diving board. "Poetry in motion," Sam said, eyeing Kurt's retreating form.

"I'll second that," Emma said with a grin.

"Hey, guess what I did this morning," Sam said, sitting up so she could put her hair in a ponytail. "I mailed in my application to find my birth parents." Sam had told Emma and Carrie all about the organization.

"Great!" Carrie said. "How long will it be before you hear from them?"

Sam shrugged. "They're supposed to call within a few days of getting the application. And after that it just depends on the case. . . ." She squinted up at the sun. "You think I need sun block or am I dark enough to go without?"

"You should always use some sun block," Emma said.

Sam flipped the bottle of sunscreen to Carrie. "Get my back?"

Carrie squirted the sunscreen into her hand and rubbed it onto Sam's back. "So, I guess it could take a while before they really have any info for you, huh?"

"It could happen right away, too," Sam said. "It's going to be so incredible. I bet my mother is this tall, foxy redhead who looks just like me!"

"Maybe," Emma said softly.

"Maybe she's even a professional dancer or something, wouldn't that be outrageous?" Sam said, taking the sunscreen from Carrie. "I mean, where did I get my looks from? And my talent? It's got to be from her."

"Maybe," Carrie said.

Sam looked at her two friends. "What is it with the two of you? Aren't I allowed to get excited about this? Or is it just that you guys can't imagine what it would be like to not even know your own mother?"

"I guess we can't really," Carrie agreed.

"We *are* excited for you," Emma said. "We just don't want you to expect too much."

"Now, this is something I have always failed to understand about both of you," Sam said. "Believe it or not, getting excited is a good thing, not a bad thing!"

"Sure," Carrie allowed. "All we're saying is if they do help you find your birth mother, don't expect too much."

"God, you're so negative," Sam chided. "It's really a drag." She pulled her sunglasses down and lay back on the towel to soak up the rays.

Emma and Carrie were silent for a moment. "Did you tell your parents that you're doing this?" Carrie finally asked.

"No," Sam said, her eyes closed behind her sunglasses.

"Don't you think it would be a good idea?" Carrie ventured.

Sam sat up on one elbow and faced Carrie. "Hey, it would have been a good idea for them to mention to me that I'd been adopted in the first place, but they didn't."

"I know," Carrie said, which mollified Sam enough so that she lay back down on her lounge chair.

"Look, I'll mention it next time I talk to them, okay?" Sam finally said.

"Hey, how's it going?" called a short, eager-faced guy who had just walked up to them. It was Howie Lawrence, who had a huge crush on Carrie. "Look who I dragged to the club with me!" he said. What was really weird was that the guy he had "dragged to the club" with him was Billy Sampson, Carrie's boyfriend.

"Well, hi there," Carrie said, with a dubious note to her voice.

"Hi," Billy said in his low, sexy voice.

"Billy's my guest today," Howie explained.

"Seems like a nice place," Billy said, looking around at the opulent country club. "Not exactly my style, though."

Sam had to smile at that. He did look a little out of place in his sun-bleached cutoffs, with his long hair flowing around his face and the diamond stud twinkling in his ear.

"I thought it would be cool if we all hung out, you know?" Howie said, attempting a casual tone. He sat on the edge of Carrie's lounge chair.

"Well, sure," Carrie said, not sounding sure at all. Howie was terribly jealous of Billy, but apparently was trying to improve his somewhat nerdy image by hanging out with him.

"How about if I order a pizza and have them bring it out by the pool?" Howie suggested, standing up. "What's everyone like on it?"

"They have a fit if you eat pizza out here," Carrie said.

"My dad's president of the board of the club this year," Howie said, looking at Carrie to see if she was impressed. "That ought to count for something. I'll go check it out."

Billy sat down on the spot that Howie had vacated. He leaned over and kissed Carrie lightly. "You look great," he said.

"Thanks," Carrie said, smiling at him seductively.

"Please, none of that in my presence," Sam chided, "it's hot enough out here."

"I wanted to ask you something about the auditions," Carrie said to Billy. "Claudia has this great new video camera that she said I could borrow. I was thinking it would be cool to video the audition, you know, sort of a cinema verité of the audition process."

"What's that mean?" Sam asked, peering over her sunglasses.

"It means the film is real life, not scripted," Carrie explained.

"Hey, sounds good to me, then!" Sam said. "I get to play myself!"

"It's cool with me if you tape it," Billy told Carrie. "I'll have to run it by the other guys, but I don't think anyone will care."

"Billy Sampson!" Becky screeched, running over to the group. Allie ran alongside her sister.

Oh, great, Sam thought to herself. *The*

monsters do show up at all the best moments.

Sam noticed that the twins had taken off the oversize T-shirts they'd been wearing in the car. Now they sported tiny yellow bikinis made mostly of fishnet.

"Remember us?" Allie asked Billy. "We're two of the Flirts' biggest fans."

"Great," Billy said with an easy smile.

Sam wondered if Billy remembered that Allie and Becky were the kids that she took care of. She couldn't tell by his face.

"We're really looking forward to the auditions tomorrow," Becky said. She flipped her long hair over her shoulder and gave Billy her most coy look.

"Yeah," Allie agreed. "Don't you think twins would look awesome singing and dancing behind you guys?"

"Wearing bikinis?" Becky added.

Billy laughed. "Well, bikinis aren't really what I had in mind."

"Wouldn't you guys like to go take a swim or something?" Sam asked them pointedly.

The twins ignored her and preened for Billy.

"Maybe no bikinis, then," Becky said. "But what should we wear to the audition?"

Billy shrugged. "Anything you feel comfortable in, I guess. Tomorrow everyone will be dancing, not singing, if that makes any difference to you."

Billy definitely doesn't remember who the twins are, Sam thought to herself. *He has no idea that they're only fourteen.*

"Uh, Billy—" Sam began.

"So we'll see you at the audition," Allie said, shooting Sam a smug look.

"Sure," Billy said. "Good luck."

"Hey, you guys are not auditioning," Sam said.

"He just said we could," Becky snapped at Sam.

"That's because he doesn't remember that you're only fourteen."

"You're fourteen?" Billy asked them.

The twins shot Sam a look that could kill. "Just ignore her," Allie advised. "She's just jealous of us."

"Hey, sorry, girls, but fourteen's a little too young," Billy said.

The twins stared hard at Sam. "I hate you," Becky seethed. Then she turned around and ran toward the club house. Allie ran after her.

"What was that all about?" Carrie asked.

"I remember them now," Billy said, snapping his fingers. "Those are the kids you take care of, right, Sam?"

"Evidently I'm not doing too good a job," Sam said ruefully. "They're a mess."

"Maybe you shouldn't have said they were fourteen in front of everybody," Emma suggested kindly. "I think you really embarrassed them."

"You're probably right," Sam groaned. "But they drive me nuts!"

"Okay, pizza delivery is all set," Howie said, walking up to the group. "Hey, I just saw the Jacobs twins leaving with Harley and Frank McFee on their motorcycles," he told Sam. "Those guys are bad news."

"Who the hell are they?" Sam asked.

"Two locals, really bad guys. They're at least in their early twenties," Howie said. "They work here in the kitchen."

"Oh, damn," Sam said, jumping up. "I've got to stop them."

"Too late," Howie said. "They were roaring out of the parking lot when I walked over here."

"I'm totally screwed," Sam said, putting her head in her hands.

"They'll probably just ride around and

then go home," Carrie said in a comforting voice.

Sam looked at the circle of her concerned friends. "I have a really bad feeling about this," she said, standing up. "I'm going to go call their dad."

As Sam headed for the pay phone, her hands were shaking. Dan Jacobs wasn't known for his excellent parenting, but he did have a lot of faith in Sam. And right now she felt that whatever the twins were up to, it was all her fault.

FOUR

"Maybe we should call the police," Sam suggested to Mr. Jacobs for about the tenth time in two hours.

It was one o'clock in the morning, and the twins still had not been heard from since leaving the country club with Harley and Frank McFee. When Sam had called Mr. Jacobs, he'd told her not to worry, that the twins were very mature for their age and he was sure they were okay. Well, that had been more than twelve hours ago, and Sam was really starting to freak out.

"They're good girls," Dan Jacobs said, almost as if he were trying to convince himself. "They should have called, but time gets away from you when you're young . . ."

Sam felt like taking him by the shoulders

and shaking some sense into him. It was so crazy! The summer before when Sam had started working for him, he'd been overprotective toward the twins. Now he erred to the other extreme.

"Time did not get away from them for twelve hours," Sam pointed out. Her stomach flip-flopped with anxiety. *Where are they? If only I hadn't embarrassed them in front of everyone!*

Dan paced the den and looked out the front windows for about the hundredth time. "If we don't hear from them in . . . let's say fifteen minutes, I'll call the police," he finally decided.

"Something is going on with them," Sam said, "I don't know what."

"I do," Dan said with a sigh, running his hand wearily over the day's growth of beard on his face. He sat heavily on the couch. "They got a letter from their mother."

"From their mother?" Sam echoed in shock. The twins' mother had left them many years ago—allegedly she'd run off with a younger man. To Sam's knowledge, no one had heard from her since.

"Yes, not that she's earned the title," Dan said bitterly. "She said she thinks about them and she loves them and someday she hopes they'll understand why she did what she did."

"Was there a return address?" Sam asked.

"No," Dan said. "The postmark was somewhere in Michigan." He looked up at Sam. "What could have possessed her to write to them? She hasn't contacted them in years."

"That's what I thought," Sam said, sitting on the leather chair near the couch.

"And to write the letter and then not give them an address . . . it's damn cruel!" Mr. Jacobs added bitterly.

"It is," Sam agreed quietly. She thought about her own search for her birth mother. What if she turned out to be as irresponsible as the twins' mother? What if she didn't even want to know Sam? But as quickly as the thought came, Sam blocked it out of her mind. Surely her own mother was nothing like that.

"Did you ever think about getting the twins some professional help?" Sam ventured. "I mean, just someone to talk to about all this . . ."

"They talk to you," Mr. Jacobs aid.

"Well, yeah," Sam agreed, shifting uncomfortably. She didn't feel competent to be the "adult" that the twins talked to. *They definitely need someone who knows more than I do*, Sam thought. But before she could say anything else, she heard the roaring of two motorcycles turning into their driveway.

"Thank God," Mr. Jacobs murmured as he opened the front door for his two daughters.

"Bye!" Allie called, waving to the guys on the motorcycles as they revved out of the driveway. She turned to look over at her father. "You didn't need to wait up, Daddy, dear."

"Neither did you, Sam, dear," Becky added, moving into the front hall.

"Do you girls realize what time it is?" Mr. Jacobs asked his daughters.

"Late, I guess," Becky said carelessly, heading for the stairs. Allie walked right behind her.

For a moment Sam thought that their father was just going to let them go upstairs without saying another word. But just as the twins hit the third step, he seemed to find his voice.

"Go into the den, both of you," he said. "We need to have a talk."

Allie sighed dramatically, but she came back down the stairs and headed for the den.

"Bor-ing," Becky singsonged, and walked around Sam to flop into the leather chair. Sam smelled liquor on her breath.

"You girls left the club without saying a word to Sam, and you've been gone all day and all night," Mr. Jacobs said. "Not a phone call, nothing."

"Gee, we lost track of the time," Allie said. Her tone of voice made it clear that she was lying and she didn't care who knew it.

"Do you have any idea how worried Sam and I have been about you?" he asked. Sam thought Mr. Jacobs looked as if he were about to cry.

"Oh, I didn't know we needed to worry about the hired help, dad," Becky said.

Their father was quiet for a moment, shaking his head. He clearly was in over his head. "This is inexcusable behavior," he finally said. "The two of you are grounded."

"Okay," Allie said. "Is that it?"

"You're grounded for a week," he added. "I mean it. Right, Sam?"

"Right," Sam answered dutifully. *But what I really want to do is call a time-out and start this whole conversation again,* Sam thought. *He's handling this all wrong!*

"Sam is backing me up on this, girls," Mr.

Jacobs warned, "so don't try to get around her." He looked uncertainly at Sam. "But . . . if you need someone, uh, female to talk to, I'm sure Sam will listen. Right, Sam?"

"Right," Sam answered again.

"We have absolutely nothing to say to her," Allie sneered contemptuously. "Come on, Becky." The twins turned their backs on their father and Sam, and went up to their room.

"I mean it," Mr. Jacobs said. "They are really grounded."

"Days and nights?" Sam asked.

"All the time," Dan said firmly. "They can't go to the club or the beach, and they can't have friends over, either."

"Okay," Sam said. "I'll do my best." She got up to go to bed, then turned back to her employer. "I'm supposed to go to the Play Café tomorrow afternoon—remember, I told you about the auditions for the backup singers . . ."

Mr. Jacobs nodded. "You can go. I'd like to spend some time with them tomorrow anyway, as a family. Maybe it'll help."

"I hope so," Sam said. "I'm glad they're okay, at least."

"Me, too," Mr. Jacobs said. "And, Sam, thanks for caring."

48

Sam went up to her room and undressed for bed. This was just too crazy. He hadn't even asked his fourteen-year-old daughters what they'd been doing with those two low-lifes until one o'clock in the morning!

I'm not their mother, Sam told herself as she fell into bed. *I can't fix what's wrong in this house. It's not my problem.* But even as she turned over and began to drift off to sleep, she knew she cared much more than she wanted to admit.

"Get down, Emma, you look hot!" Sam crowed the next afternoon when she spotted Emma coming into the Play Café.

Sam had just arrived for the Flirts' auditions. Her stomach fluttered nervously but she was not about to let on to anyone, certainly not to Emma.

"Are you sure this is okay?" Emma asked, looking down at herself. She had on baggie white shorts held up by a braided leather belt, and a hot pink and white lycra bra top. "I never did anything like this before in my life!"

"It's fine," Sam assured her. "Very you, sexy and understated."

A girl in oversize sunglasses pushed by

them and walked into the club. She was wearing an acid green spandex number with thin straps that ran up the center of her breasts, and nothing underneath it.

"Maybe understated wasn't the right fashion choice," Emma said ruefully, watching the girl walk confidently into the club.

"Trust me, she's trying too hard," Sam said, opening the door of the club. "Not that I wouldn't give up a week's salary to see Princess Cresswell of the yachting set parade around in a uni like that!"

"Very funny," Emma said as she scanned the crowd of girls milling around the club. "There must be forty girls here," Emma cried. "I never should have said I'd do this."

"Hi, you two!" Carrie said, coming up to them from the back of the club. "I was just getting some video on the guys before this starts. They're really psyched about the turnout."

"I should leave," Emma murmured.

"No, you shouldn't," Sam said firmly.

"I could just sit and watch, or I could help you with your video, Carrie," Emma pleaded.

"You're going to be great," Carrie told Emma. "You dance really well, and you're a terrific singer—I've heard you singing along in the car lots of times!"

"I was in choirs at school in Switzerland," Emma allowed, "but I don't know . . ."

"Hey, you've got the best voice of the three of us, by far!" Carrie told her.

"Thanks a lot," Sam said, dropping her oversize bag on a table.

"Oops," Carrie said meekly. "Well, you can dance rings around us," Carrie said, trying to make up for her gaffe.

"I can sing," Sam insisted. She pulled off her sweatshirt and stepped out of her jeans. "Well?" Sam asked, spinning around for their benefit.

"You look unbelievable," Carrie said.

"You do," Emma agreed. "Is that new?"

Sam looked down at her extra high cut white lace spandex leotard. The front had a high neck, but the back was cut down below her waistline. The effect was simple and devastatingly sexy. "Yeah, it's new," Sam confessed.

"Whatever you paid for it was worth it," Carrie assured her.

Emma looked around at some of the overly made-up, practically naked girls.

"Now I see what you mean about trying too hard," she said. "You look much hotter."

"Why, Sammi, don't you look sweet in white," Lorell purred, seemingly appearing out of nowhere. "Might as well enjoy it now," she added, "I don't think you'll be wearing that color on your wedding day."

"Yeah, like you will," Sam snorted at her.

"Just a teensy fashion tip," Lorell continued, "but everyone knows that redheads shouldn't wear white. It just washes you out, poor thing!"

Sam rolled her eyes. She might be a redhead, but she was a redhead who tanned, and at the moment her tan was as dark as Lorell's.

"Hi, girls," Diana said, coming up to the group.

Sam gulped hard. It was bad enough that Lorell looked so cute in her electric blue tights and bra top, but Diana looked awesome in a simple low-cut emerald-green leotard. *Let's face it*, Sam thought glumly to herself, *she's got body of death, and a bust line to die for. No one that ugly on the inside should look that beautiful on the outside.*

"Why, Emma," Diana said, her eyes taking

in Emma's outfit, "don't tell me you're going to audition. You might actually sweat!"

"Hi!" Billy's voice boomed through a microphone set up on the stage. "I'm Billy Sampson—"

"We know!" a female voice yelled out from the crowd. Everyone laughed.

"Well, yeah, I guess you do," Billy answered with a grin. "Anyway, we want to thank you all for coming. This is a great turnout."

"I'm going to get the video camera," Carrie whispered, and scooted away from the group.

"What we're gonna do," Billy continued, "is start with the dance auditions today, then if you make the cut you'll sing next time." Billy looked around the stage. "Where's Tisha?" he asked. An attractive young black woman with a great body made her way onto the stage. "Everybody, this is Tisha Petrie," he said, putting his arm around her shoulders. "She does the choreography for the Boston Celtics' cheerleaders," he added. A murmur of excitement ran through the crowd. "Tisha is going to run the show today, so I'll turn this over to her."

"Hi," the young woman said into the microphone. "What the guys tell me they're looking for is three girls who can really move, as well as really sing. We're not talking step-touch-turn here, but real get-down choreography. Now, you don't need to be intimidated by that," she cautioned, "just follow the directions I give you. Some girls just have a lot of natural talent for this, and that can make up for the training."

"I was hoping I could just look cute and shimmy," a girl in the crowd joked nervously.

"Sorry," Tisha said. "If that's what the guys wanted, then they wasted their money by hiring me today. Okay, what we're going to do is play the demo of the Flirts' 'Hot Night' through the sound system. I'll show you all a combination of steps, and then you'll come up here in groups of three and take a crack at it."

"I can't do this!" Emma whispered frantically to Sam.

"Sure you can!" Sam encouraged her.

Tisha nodded and someone turned on the sound system. "I'll run through it with the music first," Tisha told them.

The sounds of "Hot Night" blasted through the air. Tisha began dancing, her sinewy arms reaching out, her muscular legs high kicking into the air.

"This is like something out of a Janet Jackson video!" Emma whispered to Sam. "I'm out of here!"

Sam put her hand on Emma's arm. "Watch carefully," she said. "She's going to break it down, and then it won't seem so overwhelming. It's really not that hard."

To Sam's great relief, the combinations really were fairly simple. In fact, her audition for Disney World had been much tougher. She felt her confidence increase as she watched the choreographer dance.

"That's it," Tisha said cheerfully when she finished. "Now I'll show it to you without the music. Can everybody see?"

The group jockeyed for position in the room, staring up intently.

"Okay, we'll be starting on the chorus, where Billy sings 'It's gonna be a hot night, baby, tonight,'" Tisha explained. "One, two, one, two, three, four," she counted off her beginning combination. "And cross-step, snap! Cross-step, snap! Pelvic thrust, isolation, hip roll, and turn!"

"What is she talking about?" Emma moaned.

"It doesn't matter if you know the names," Sam said. "Keep your eyes glued to her. All you have to do is copy her. Count it off in your head." Sam leaned in to Emma and counted. "See how her hips went out? Watch again—she does it every time the lyric goes 'hot night.' See?"

Emma nodded, a look of intense concentration on her face. "I see. That helps," she said, nodding.

"Okay, let's all try it together," Tisha said from the stage. "Space yourselves out there, ladies."

The group moved apart to allow them some room to dance. Pres flicked the music back on.

Sam watched Emma out of the corner of her eye. Emma was getting about half of the moves right. *Not bad for starters*, she thought.

"The hip goes out on 'to-night,' every time," Sam whispered, "the snap comes on the word 'baby.'"

Emma nodded and added the two moves during the next combination.

"Now you're getting it!" Sam encouraged her friend.

"I think I kind of am!" Emma said. She began to move with more confidence, making all the difference in the world.

Hey, she looks really good, Sam said to herself. *What if she gets it instead of me?*

"That was good," Tisha told the group. "Let's give it a go. Please pick up a number off the table over there, and pin it on your outfit so we can keep track of you. Now let's have three brave women up here to start."

Sam, Emma, and a slender brunette made up the fourth group. As they hit the stage Carrie turned on the video camera. "Good luck," she called.

"Piece of cake," Sam said, trying to look sexy and confident.

The music to "Hot Night" filled the air once again. Sam danced for all she was worth. She knew she got it right, and looked good, too. Emma seemed to be hanging right in there too. The brunette was hopeless.

"Great," Tisha said to Sam as she came off stage. "You must have had training."

"I have danced professionally," Sam told her.

"It shows," the choreographer said, making a note on her pad. "Okay, next group!" she called out.

"Did you hear that? Did you hear that?"

Sam asked Emma as they came off stage. "She really thought I was good!"

"Well, of course she did!" Emma said. "I just wonder if I looked like a fool."

"You were fabulous," Sam told her loyally. "Hey, look who just hit the stage."

Diana and Lorell were both in the next threesome. The music started up and they began dancing.

"Oh, my God, she's great," Sam muttered, her heart sinking.

"You mean Diana?" Emma said with a sigh, watching Diana move. "I'm afraid you're right."

Sam looked over at Tisha, who was nodding her head and making more notes.

"I will die if she gets in this with me," Sam hissed.

"They wouldn't really ever hire Diana, would they?" Emma asked.

"Not if I have anything to say about it," Sam muttered. She looked over at Pres as he watched the dancers intently from across the room. "Excuse me while I go use my considerable influence," she said, and headed straight for him.

FIVE

Beep beep. Beep beep. Beep beep . . .
Sam's alarm clock sounded insistently at her
for nearly a minute before she reached a
sleepy hand over and snapped it off.

Sam barely opened her eyes to look at the
time. *Six forty-five in the morning. No one
should be awake at six forty-five in the
morning, especially me.* She fumbled to
turn off the alarm and go back to sleep, but
then she remembered why she had set it.
The night before Kurt had called and invited
her, along with the entire gang, to go white-
water canoeing with him. Although she had
no deep desire to shoot the rapids in some
flimsy craft, Kurt had mentioned that he'd
already invited Pres, and Pres had already
accepted. Since she'd parted so badly with

Pres at the Play Café, she jumped at the chance to see him and get everything straightened out.

She turned over and stared at the ceiling, remembering what had happened at the auditions. Pres had been friendly, in a remote kind of way. Sam had leaned over to see what he'd written about Diana, and he'd moved the paper away.

"Hey," Sam had said, "Diana isn't actually in the running here, is she?"

And Pres had said, "I can't talk with you about this now and you know it."

"Well, excuse me," Sam had said and had walked away. She was loathe to admit that she hadn't had nearly the influence on Pres that she'd hoped.

Sam threw back the covers and headed for the shower, hoping it would wake her up.

As the hot water cascaded down her face, she remembered that she had actually been dreaming about Pres. In her dream, she had seen him as a young boy with two women on one side of him and two men on the other side. They'd been walking toward her, and she'd been just about to say something to him when her alarm had woken her up. *The adults are his adoptive parents and his biological parents—even I can figure that out—but what was I going to say?* Sam made a mental note to tell Pres about her dream later in the day.

Sam quickly towel dried and pulled out some clothes. She chose a faded pair of jeans, a Harvard sweatshirt from some old boyfriend, and a pair of pink high-tops. Kurt had warned her about getting sunburned out on the river, and about how sneakers would come in handy if she had to jump out of the canoe into the river. "Perish the thought," she'd joked. "I don't jump into rivers. Pres'll save me!" She raced downstairs, made a quick cup of coffee, and was out the door. Kurt's borrowed Jeep, filled with her friends, was already waiting in the Jacobses' driveway.

"You promise you'll have me back here by four P.M., O great white explorer?" Sam jokingly asked Kurt as she climbed into the backseat. "Because Mr. Jacobs only gave me the time off until four—he's 'bonding' with the monsters until then," she added, rolling her eyes.

"No problem, sailor," Kurt said with a grin. "I'll have you back here in plenty of time . . . if you don't get struck by the Saco River curse."

"Say what?" Sam asked, snuggling against Pres, who put his arm around her warmly.

Hmm, she thought, *I guess he's not too ticked at me after all.*

Kurt gunned the Jeep and headed for the ferry. "You don't know about the curse?" he asked. "Some Indian medicine man of the Ossipee tribe supposedly put a curse on the river," he explained.

"Oh, come on," Carrie chided from the other side of Pres.

"I speak the truth," Kurt answered solemnly, pulling the Jeep onto the ferry ramp. "The curse was that no white men were supposed to be able to canoe the whole thing without encountering mortal danger."

"We've got some hellified curses down in Tennessee," Pres drawled as the ferry pulled away from the dock, "but I just don't like to repeat 'em in mixed company."

"Believe me," Emma said, "every curse you know, Sam already knows. In fact, Sam probably invented them," she added with a laugh.

"Hey, what happened with the twins yesterday, anyway?" Carrie asked Sam as the ferry took off.

Sam proceeded to relate the latest saga to her friends. "It's not a pretty story," she concluded.

"Those kids really need to get themselves together," Carrie said, shaking her head.

Sam agreed. She knew her friends would understand better if she told them about the letter the twins had received from their mom, but somehow that felt like breaking a confidence, so she didn't say anything. *Anyway*, she thought to herself, snuggling closer to Pres, *I'm glad good ole dad is with them this morning instead of me.* Sam closed her eyes contentedly and fell fast asleep.

"Hey, Sam, get up! We're here!" Emma's voice, warm but insistent, cut through her slumber.

"What?" Sam asked, rubbing sleep from her eyes for the second time that morning and looking around groggily. They were obviously at some sort of canoeing rental center. "What time is it?"

"Time to hit the water," Kurt replied. "We're already at the river. You slept for an hour. We'll leave the Jeep here and take these rental canoes downstream." He pointed to three aluminum canoes nearby. "After lunch, we'll run the rapids at East Lemington bridge, and then get picked up by the outfitter's van. He'll bring us back here to get the Jeep."

Billy and Pres were already hard at work, getting life vests for everyone, securing lunches in the bottom of the canoes, and choosing paddles. Pres even loaded some freshwater fishing gear and pinned a one-day fishing license to his vest.

"Okay," Sam said, getting out of the Jeep and stretching. "I'm ready for this."

"Listen up, you guys," Kurt said, getting their attention. "I know that Pres and Billy have run rapids before, so they'll be in the stern of the canoes, steering. I'll take Emma with me, Carrie'll go with Billy, and Sam goes with Pres."

"You're my bowman, er, bowperson." Pres smiled at her, lashing the last of their gear to the canoe.

"Why do I get stuck with *him*?" Sam joked, pointing at Pres with mock disappointment.

"Because you begged to get stuck with him," Kurt reminded her. "Too late to change now. Okay, put on those life jackets, and we'll paddle out and give you girls a canoeing lesson."

"Uh, Kurt?" Carrie asked, fixing her vest carefully.

"Yeah?"

"I've done this before. About a hundred times. My family has an Old Town."

Kurt looked chagrined. "Oops," he said.

"Oops is right," she said, half teasing and half serious.

"Tell you what, then," Kurt decided. "I'll work with Emma, you teach Sam."

"No way!" Sam cried. "Not her!" They all cracked up.

"She's impossible, folks," Pres said, sliding his arm around Sam, "we either got to love her or kill her."

"Should we take a vote?" Emma quipped.

They climbed into their canoes and paddled out to the middle of the river. Carrie and Billy maneuvered their canoes alongside Pres and Sam's, and it wasn't long before Sam was stroking confidently from the bow, with Pres steering from the stern.

Sam looked behind her and saw that Emma was doing just fine, too. The three couples paddled easily downstream, enjoying the feeling of riding along on the current. Sam knew that they were not far from civilization, but out here, on the river, she could pretend that she was somewhere in the wilderness.

"Hey, Pres," she joked, continuing to do the bow stroke that Carrie had taught her, "why don't you and I make a little detour down that small stream over there? We'll catch up with the rest of them later."

"Because knowing you, sweet thing," Pres shot back, "we'd never get back in time to meet them!" Pres cocked his head for a moment, as if listening for something.

"What are you doing?" Sam asked.

"Hear that?" Pres asked her.

"Hear what?" Sam turned her head from side to side. All she could hear was the wind picking up.

"That's no l'il ol' breeze," Pres answered, a grin starting to spread across his face. "That's the sound of white water." And he let out a rebel yell that echoed from shore to shore.

Pres was right. As they rounded the next bend in the river, the sound got even louder. They were on a long, straight stretch of the Saco, and about a quarter mile ahead, Sam could see the pace of the current quickening, as it splashed over rocks and zoomed into a narrow gorge.

It was the rapids!

Kurt and Emma's canoe was in the lead, and Sam watched as Kurt slowed the craft to a standstill near a sandbar on one bank. Pres and Billy each steered to a stop right next to Kurt.

"Okay!" said Kurt. He was as psyched as Pres was. "This is our first set of rips. Pres, Billy, and Carrie have done this before. They know that to keep control of your canoe, you have to paddle faster than the water. So Sam and Emma, when you get to the rapids, paddle like the dickens. If you flip, get away from the boat, and let the current carry you downstream."

"Oh, no!" Sam cried. "I could die before I'm famous!" Her friends cracked up.

"No," Billy corrected her gently. "You'll get a sore butt before you're famous." They all laughed again.

"Let's do it!" Carrie cried. Two at a time, they started paddling toward the rapids. Sam and Pres were second in line and made sure to leave ample space in front of them for Kurt and Emma's canoe. Sam looked on, astonished, as the first boat sped up and then disappeared into the splashing white water and rushing torrents of the rapids.

Then, she saw them again, several hundred yards downstream. They were through!

"Our turn," Pres said to her, his experienced eye picking out a course through the rips. "Let's tear these puppies up!"

Sam started paddling faster. She could feel the quickening current pressing them into the rapids now. Huge boils of water were all around her as the river rushed over submerged rocks and shot through narrow chutes. "Yeeow!" Sam cried. "We're jamming!" The canoe slapped against a bunch of standing waves that felt to Sam like aquatic speedbumps, and water splashed all over her.

And then they were through. Pres maneuvered the canoe so they could watch Billy and Carrie, and Sam watched in amazement as their friends slid through the rapids at an almost unbelievable speed.

"Did we look like that?" she asked Pres excitedly.

"Better than that," Pres answered, smiling. "You were in the bow."

Sam grinned. *This is the greatest*, she thought.

The group canoed on for a few miles, running eight more sets of rapids. Sam and Pres banged a rock pretty hard on one set, but no harm was done.

"I'm starved!" Sam said, resting for a moment and letting Pres and the current do the work. "What time is it?"

"Nearly noon," Pres answered.

"Noon! I haven't eaten for five hours. I'm going to wither away," Sam said dramatically, letting her hand trail in the water.

"Naah," Pres replied, pointing up ahead. "I think we're stopping for lunch." Ahead of them, Kurt was aiming his canoe toward another of the river's many sandbars.

"We're stopping here!" Kurt yelled back. "We'll eat, then the East Lemington rapids are just half a mile ahead."

It wasn't long before all three canoes were safely up on the sandbar, and Emma and Kurt spread out a fabulous picnic lunch. For a time, all six friends ate contentedly, not saying a word. Sam and Pres had found a shady spot away from the others, and Sam was leaning her head into Pres's lap as she virtually inhaled a peanut butter sandwich.

69

"Know what?" Pres asked languidly.

"Mmm—what?" Sam asked back, the peanut butter sticking to the roof of her mouth.

"I love the taste of peanut butter," Pres replied, pressing his lips gently against hers.

Sam smiled. "Well, I must say, you're a whole lot friendlier now than you were yesterday."

"That was work," Pres said, "this is play."

"You acted like you hardly knew me," Sam said.

"Hey, I don't think that's true," Pres said, lifting a lock of hair off her face.

"You wouldn't really hire Diana, would you?" Sam asked.

"You know, that question is gettin' a mite tired," Pres said.

"Meaning you're not going to answer it?" Sam replied.

Pres leaned over and kissed her. "Meaning you're right."

Sam sighed. "Well, can you at least tell me if I was good, or is that top secret, too?"

"You were great," Pres said. "You're really talented."

"I wonder where I got it from," Sam mused, plucking a long blade of grass and sticking it between her lips. "Maybe my real mom is a dancer or something."

"Any word yet from F.F.A., my fellow adoptee?"

Sam shook her head. "It's only been a couple of days, though. I can't wait."

"Just don't expect too much," Pres cautioned her.

"That's what Emma and Carrie keep saying," Sam said. She tickled Pres's cheek with the blade of grass. "But you of all people must know how I feel."

Pres nodded. "I've often thought about putting in an application. But something always stops me. I've been told the whole thing can be pretty frustrating."

"That won't happen to me," Sam said. "I just know it won't."

"Just remember, all kinds of things can go wrong," Pres reminded her. "And once you meet your birth parents, they might not be who you've made up in your mind they're going to be."

"Yes, Dr. Pres," Sam said gravely. "Send me a bill for the session."

"I'll take it out in trade," he murmured into her neck.

* * *

The rest of the outing passed in a whirlwind of fun. They finished lunch and then navigated the treacherous East Lemington rapids without getting struck by Kurt's "curse." Sam was deposited at the Jacobses' right at four o'clock. She said good-bye to her friends, kissed Pres for the last time that day, and headed up the walkway to the house.

The twins were there to greet her.

"Hey, Sam," Allie said, even before Sam could get through the door, "what's the difference between Becky and a pig?"

Here we go again, Sam said to herself.

"About two ounces!" Allie hooted with glee.

"Allie, you are so queer!" Becky retorted. "You're too stupid to remember we're not talking to her."

Sam sighed. She was used to the twins being obnoxious, but this was getting ridiculous. "Look, do you guys want to talk or anything?" she asked them.

"I just said we're not speaking to you," Becky said.

"Well, if you change your mind, it's okay," Sam said gently.

"Never happen," Allie said smugly.

"Look, I know about the letter from your mom," Sam said. "Your dad told me."

"How dare he?" Becky screamed. "It's none of your business."

"He's worried about you," Sam said. "And so am I."

"Oh, sure, I really buy that one," Allie snorted. "Come on, Becky, let's go upstairs where we can have some privacy." The twins flounced away.

The phone rang shrilly and Sam picked it up in the kitchen.

"Jacobs residence."

"May I speak to Samantha Bridges?"

"Speaking," Sam answered. She had no idea who it could be.

"This is Audrey Birnbaum, from the Family Finders Agency," she said.

"Oh, yes!" Sam replied, clutching the phone tighter.

"We received your application today," Ms. Birnbaum said, "and we'd like to be able to get started on your case. Unfortunately you didn't provide us with very much information."

"I—I guess I don't *have* very much information," Sam admitted.

"Perhaps your adoptive parents could be of help," Ms. Birnbaum suggested.

"Maybe," Sam said dubiously.

"Have you told them you're going through this process?" Ms. Birnbaum asked.

"Not really," Sam admitted. "I don't know how they'd take it."

"Well, I can understand that," the warm voice replied. "But it might be a good idea. They may have more information, and in the long run, they'll be more hurt if this gets sprung on them than if they knew all along, don't you think?"

"I suppose," Sam agreed reluctantly.

"You make your own choices on it," Ms. Birnbaum said. "But it really would be much easier for us if you could tell us the exact date of your adoption, and any information your parents might have concerning your birth parents."

"I'll try," Sam said. She thanked Ms. Birnbaum for calling and hung up.

Great, Sam thought, staring at the phone. *I really feel like calling my parents to tell them about this. I'll do it later*, she decided, wanting to put it off as long as possible.

But from upstairs Sam heard "shut up,

you douche bag!" and some equally horrid reply.

"On second thought, I'd rather face my parents than the monsters," she said out loud, and picked up the phone.

She took a deep breath, crossed her fingers, and dialed her home number in Kansas.

SIX

"Hello," came Sam's mother's voice through the phone.

"Hi, Mom, it's me," Sam said, "calling from Maine."

"Oh, hi, Sam!" her mother said, a note of false happiness entering her voice.

This is going to be a barrel of laughs, I can tell already, Sam thought. *How can such a great day turn into such a horrible one so quickly?*

Ever since Sam had found out that she was adopted, she couldn't seem to have a normal conversation with her parents. And her mother always seemed to be forcing herself to be cheerful, as if she was afraid all the time of what could be said.

"How come you're calling? Is everything okay?" Mrs. Bridges asked.

Well, here goes. Break it to her gently,
Sam reminded herself. "Mom, I've sort of
been thinking . . ." Sam started.

"About what?" Mrs. Bridges asked.

"About my adoption," Sam said, trying to
control what she thought was an obvious
nervousness to her voice.

"Well, of course," Mrs. Bridges said. "Of
course you've been thinking about it. We've
been thinking about it, too. That's what that
therapist on your island suggested that we
do."

After Sam had learned she was adopted,
she and her parents had met with a family
therapist who summered on Sunset Island.
Sam had actually found it somewhat helpful.

Here goes, Sam thought. "Well, the thing
is, Mom, I—I want to meet my real parents."

Silence from her mother. Sam winced.
She heard what she'd just said echoing in
her mind. Real parents, that's what she'd
said, as if the parents that had raised her
were her fake parents. But some angry part
of Sam didn't want to offer her mother
reassurances, so she didn't.

Finally her mother spoke. "How long have
you been thinking about this?"

Sam doodled on a sheet of paper as she spoke. "Since the moment I learned I was adopted, Mom."

"I see," Mrs. Bridges replied. Sam could hear the whine of a lawn mower over the phone. "Your father's out cutting the grass," she added.

"Is that relevant?" Sam asked. She knew how her mother always seemed to defer to her father, and it annoyed her.

"I wish he were on the phone with us right now, honey," her mother said. "We talked about this possibility, of course."

"And?" Sam asked. *Maybe they're in favor of it!* she thought wildly.

"And we don't think it's a really good idea," her mother said softly.

"Yeah, well, keeping my adoption secret wasn't a real good idea, either," Sam shot back. "But I didn't have a choice that time."

Sam's mother sighed into the phone. "I know you're still angry with us, Sam. I understand that . . ."

Sam closed her eyes and tried to calm down. "This means a lot to me, Mom," she said in a low voice. "Right now this is the most important thing in my life."

"We understand that, Sam," her mother

said. "But your father and I think you should get some professional advice on this."

"I can make up my own mind! It's my life!" Sam said hotly, digging the pen into the paper.

Her mother sighed. "Yes, it is," she agreed. There was a long beat of silence, then she spoke again. "I'm going to send you your adoption file in a sealed envelope. It's got all kinds of information in it about your biological parents. If you change your mind, don't open it."

Sam breathed a sigh of relief, but at the same time a wave of anxiety and adrenaline coursed through her. *This isn't a fantasy anymore*, she thought. *I'm really going to meet them. F.F.A. will have everything they need to find them. I wish my mother would understand.*

"Sam?"

"Yes, Mom?"

"Please remember one thing. You might want to meet your biological parents, but there's no guarantee they'll want to meet you."

"Of course they will," Sam said. "Maybe you're just hoping that they won't."

"Maybe," her mother allowed. "But just

remember, whether they do or they don't, we'll love you just the same."

Sam shut her eyes, her heart a whirlwind of conflicting emotions. She loved her mother, and yet she was still so angry with her that sometimes it was hard to show the love.

"I know, Mom," Sam finally answered. "I know."

At about ten that evening, Sam walked into the Play Café, hoping that her face showed more confidence than she felt inside. The Flirts had said that they would post the first cut at nine, and Sam was feeling a little anxious.

I know I was one of the best dancers there, Sam thought to herself, *but who knows what can happen with an audition? Just because you're talented doesn't mean you're going to get picked!*

Sam walked purposefully toward the bulletin board in the back of the Play Café. It had all sorts of stuff posted on it—people looking for roommates, people looking for rides to Boston or New York, and people looking for other people.

At least I look good, Sam thought. *When*

you feel your worst, look your best, that's my rule! She had on a pair of very short denim cutoffs, a man's sleeveless white ribbed T-shirt with nothing underneath, and her famous red cowboy boots.

The bulletin board was crowded with paper, and it took Sam a moment to find the audition list. *There! At the upper left! Yes! There's my name, second on the list. Why wasn't I first? Oh, Pres probably didn't want it to look like favoritism*, she thought. *And there's Emma's name!* Sam's heart leapt, because she knew how excited Emma would be that she'd made the first cut.

Sam scanned the rest of the list quickly to see if anyone else she knew was on it. She saw Christy Powell a sexy girl who wrote for the *Breakers*. Christy had been after Pres the summer before, but this summer, to everyone's surprise, she had shown up engaged.

And then Sam saw the last name on the list, and her heart fell. It was Diana De Witt.

That unscrupulous bitch! She's only interested in doing this as a way of getting into Pres's shorts!

"Sam!" Sam heard Emma's familiar voice coming up behind her.

"Oh, hi," Sam replied dispiritedly.

"What's the matter?" Emma asked, sidling up next to her. "Don't tell me you didn't make it."

"I did make it," Sam assured her. "And so did you!"

"I did?" Emma gasped. She stepped closer to the board and looked at the list. "I really made it!" she yelped happily. "I can't believe it!"

"Look who else made it," Sam snorted in disgust, pointing to Diana De Witt's name at the end of the list. "Pres is actually going to let that bimbo continue on!"

"Hey, whatever we think of Diana, it's not fair to blame it on Pres," Emma said reasonably. "The Flirts are a band. Even if Pres didn't want her, maybe the other guys outvoted him."

"Sure," Sam retorted, her eyes still fixed on the list. "And maybe Lorell Courtland is Nancy Reagan in disguise. After all, they've never been photographed together."

"Did I hear someone say Lorell Courtland?" Sam and Emma heard a familiar voice behind them. It was Diana.

"Nah, you're hearing things again, Diana, maybe you better cut back on the tequila," Sam shot at her.

"No, I could have sworn you were talking about my friend," Diana said, her eyes scanning the list. "Not nice to gossip! Oh, here I am! Well, that's no surprise." She turned and looked Emma up and down. "Imagine your name on the list. Who would have thought it back in boarding school?"

"Emma was great," Sam snapped at Diana.

"Oh, come on," Diana said with a tinkling laugh. "Everyone knows Emma's talents run more toward seducing Aqua-Man with her credit cards!"

"Just wait," Sam told Diana. "Emma will have the last laugh when she gets this gig, and you don't."

"Sure." Diana laughed again, making it patently obvious that no such thing was possible. She looked smugly at Sam. "You know, someone would think that you're upset Pres picked me to be in the finals."

"He didn't pick you," Emma said quickly, finally finding her voice.

"Right," Sam agreed, "it was a group decision."

"Don't talk about what you don't know,

girls," Diana said lightly, her eyes challenging them to contradict her again. "Well, I'll see you two tomorrow at the next round of auditions." She turned away, then turned back once more. "Oh, Sam, just a little tip. Practice your singing. I understand you need it. Ta-ta! Don't be nervous!"

Diana turned lightly and was gone.

"What a worthless human being," said Emma when Diana had left.

"I am going to kick her butt in those auditions," Sam said meaningfully.

"I just don't understand her," Emma murmured, watching Diana walk out of the club. "I never have."

"Some people are just evil," Sam opined, "and she's one of them."

"Maybe," Emma sighed. "Carrie says she must really hate herself."

"Enough with the psycho-babble," Sam groaned. "It's simple. Diana is a bitch and she should die."

Emma laughed in spite of herself. "That's simple, all right!"

"Enough about the wicked witch of the west," Sam said, waving her hand dismissively. "You got picked and I got picked. This is very, very cool!"

"You don't think they were just being nice?" Emma asked.

"What's this? Mademoiselle Cresswell feeling insecure? Girlfriend, I'm telling you, you have natural talent."

"Believe me, this is not the sort of thing one trains for at a Swiss boarding school," Emma said loftily, making fun of her own background.

Sam hugged Emma's shoulders. "You have come so far!"

Emma laughed. "Thanks for the seal of approval. So, tomorrow we sing, right?"

"You got it," Sam agreed. "What I'd suggest is that you go home to the Hewitts' and practice singing rock backup. Because that's what I'm gonna do."

"Okay," Emma said. "For once, I'll take your advice."

When Sam got home to the Jacobs house, Mr. Jacobs was sitting alone in the living room staring out the window.

"Hi, Sam," he said as Sam wandered in. "Want to sit down a minute and chat?"

"Sure," Sam replied, plopping herself down on the love seat. "How are the twins?"

"Oh, they're okay," he said distractedly.

"They say they hate me for grounding them."

"Well, that doesn't surprise me," Sam said.

"I think it's the best thing," Mr. Jacobs told Sam earnestly, leaning forward on the couch as he spoke. "It really gives me a lot more time to be with them."

Yeah, like where were you when they really needed you? Sam thought to herself. *Like for the whole time since your wife took off? And even when you are with them, you look at them through rose-colored glasses.*

But she couldn't very well say that to her employer. Instead she said, "That's great, I'm sure it'll really give you guys a chance to, uh, bond."

"Tomorrow," Mr. Jacobs said, leaning back on the couch, "I plan to take them to Two Lights State Park. It's really pretty there. You can have the day off, until the evening anyway."

That's your concept of grounding them? Sam thought to herself. But hey, it meant she could have the time off without even having to ask for it.

"Okay," Sam said.

"You just watch," Dan continued. "In a

couple of weeks, this'll be a completely new family."

"I don't doubt it," Sam said, pasting a supportive smile on her face. "Excuse me," she added, before walking toward the stairs.

Actually, she doubted it very much.

Once upstairs and in her room, with the door tightly shut, Sam took out a small cassette player and her entire collection of tapes. She knew that if she was going to nail down a spot as a backup singer for the Flirts, she'd have to do a great job singing as well as dancing. And singing was not her long suit.

Hmmmm. What to play. Something rock and melodic. Sam picked a Michael Bolton tape and popped it into the player. Soon, she was wailing along with the backup singers at the top of her lungs. *Hey, this doesn't sound bad!* she thought to herself. She pivoted in front of the mirror and added a few moves, throwing her tumbled curls in her face and giving the mirror her sexiest expression. The bass line pounded away and she sang over it even louder, giving herself up to the music.

It wasn't until the song was over that she could tell that what she thought was a bass drum was actually someone pounding on the door of the room. She clicked the cassette off and went to answer the door.

"Geez. It sounds like someone's dying in there," Allie said, making a painful face. "You don't call that singing, do you?"

"There's no need to be nasty just because you're ticked off at me," Sam said, trying for a dignified tone.

"Believe me, this isn't nastiness," Becky said, coming up next to Allie. "That's some of the worst singing I ever heard."

"Thank you so much for that vote of support," Sam said, starting to close the door.

Allie put her foot in the door and stopped it from closing. "We just stopped by to tell you that we've already been hired to be backups for another band."

"Yeah, a better one," Becky added.

"That must have been some audition, considering that you've been grounded for days," Sam said.

"For your info, we didn't even have to audition," Becky said. "When you're hot, you're hot."

"Come on, Becky," Allie said, "let's go practice some *real* singing."

Sam shut the door and shook her head. What were the twins up to this time?

The door firmly closed, Sam turned resolutely back to the cassette player.

You do too have talent, and you are going to get picked as a backup singer, she told herself. *Now get back to work and forget about those awful monsters, and forget about Diana De Witt.*

But in her mind's eye, she had a picture of the Flirts out on tour. Billy and Pres were up front, leading the band. Emma and Diana were two of the three backup singers. And Sam wasn't there at all.

SEVEN

"How about some eggs?" Sam asked the twins the next morning as she stood in front of the refrigerator.

"Disgusting," Allie intoned. "Dead baby chicken fetuses."

"Cereal? Toast?" Sam asked.

"We're having black coffee," Becky answered, sipping from a mug that had her name in script on the side.

"Hi, girls. All ready for the park?" Mr. Jacobs asked as he walked into the kitchen.

"The girls won't eat breakfast," Sam told their father. *Geez, I feel like a broken record with this stuff,* Sam thought to herself.

"Hey, girls, breakfast is the most important meal of the day," he told his daughters.

"Yeah, but I lost another pound," Allie said.

Mr. Jacobs gave his daughter a look of approval. "Way to go, honey!" he said, reaching into the fridge for the orange juice.

Sam sighed and threw up her hands. No wonder these girls were all messed up! Their father gave them more mixed signals than any parent she'd ever seen. Well, it was their problem, not hers. She pulled a bag of English muffins out of the bread box and sliced some cheese on one for her own breakfast.

"Your singing audition is today, huh," Becky said.

"Yep," Sam confirmed, slipping the English muffin into the microwave.

"Good luck," Allie snorted. "You'll need it."

Sam turned around and looked at the twins. Mr. Jacobs had his head buried in the morning paper, and was ignoring the entire exchange.

"Look," Sam said, "I know you guys are really mad at me, and I'm sorry if I embarrassed you," Sam said. "But I really cannot take all this crap from the two of you. It ticks me off, and it hurts my feelings."

Dan looked up over the top of his newspaper. The room was quiet for a moment. He seemed to be waiting to see what his daughters would say.

"Don't make such a big deal out of it," Allie finally mumbled. She picked up her coffee cup and headed out of the kitchen, Becky trailing after her.

"They're going through a rough time . . ." Mr. Jacobs began.

"I know that," Sam said as the bell went off on the microwave. "But I'm sorry, I really can't just keep my mouth shut while they abuse me."

"I'll talk to them about it," Dan promised. He folded the paper and walked out of the kitchen.

Yeah, I'll bet, Sam thought to herself, sitting down with her solitary breakfast.

After another hour of bickering and yelling, the twins and their father left for the park, and Sam had some peace and quiet. She looked at her watch. She had two hours before the audition—just enough time to do some vocalizing and get ready. She drained the coffee from her cup and ran up to her room.

Scales. That's what the real singers at Disney World had always done to warm up, and it seemed to work for them. Sam cleared her throat and tried a tentative note, then she sang it again on "la" and proceeded to sing all the notes up the octave. Her voice sounded weak and trembly to her. She tried again. This time her voice cracked in the middle of the vocal line, switching from a chest sound to a weak little head sound.

You're just nervous, Sam told herself, pacing back and forth in her room. *Try again. Breathe deeply. From the diaphragm.* Sam remembered the singers at Disney World always talking about "vocal support" and "using the diaphragm." She had a vague idea that it meant using the lower stomach muscles, but she wasn't quite sure how.

She switched cassettes on her player and flicked on the latest Graham Perry tape. Graham's raspy voice singing "A Change Is Gonna Come" filled the room, and Sam closed her eyes and joined in on the backups.

"A change, a change is gonna come, now
  Anyday, any way I can get free now,
  Oh, baby, a change is gonna come."

"Gee, I sound great when I sing with them," she said out loud, making a face at

94

herself in the mirror. "Now if only Graham's backup singers were coming with me to this audition."

Sam jumped into the shower, vocalizing over the rushing water. The acoustics in the shower made her voice sound fuller, and she sang out lustily until the water started to get cold.

What to wear, what to wear, she mused to herself, surveying her closet. As usual half of what she owned was crumpled up on the floor, neatness not being one of her specialties. As if unconsciously remembering what Diana had said about redheads in white, she picked a black off-the-shoulder ribbed cotton top that ended in a band of lace right under the bust line. If she lifted her arms, the bottoms of her breasts would show, but she was small busted enough to get away with it. To complement the top she pulled on her oldest, most bleached-out jeans with the holes in the knees, and her trademark red cowboy boots.

Perfect, she decided, eyeing her reflection in the mirror. *You look sexy without looking like you're trying too hard.* She got out her makeup case, and put on eyeliner, mascara, and her usual red matte lipstick. Then she blow dried her hair and sprayed it into an even wilder than usual mass of red curls.

"Oh, you babe-asaurus," she told her reflection, flicking some curls over her shoulder. She picked up her purse, slung it over her shoulder, and bounded down the stairs.

Sam's self-confidence lasted until she arrived at the Play Café and walked in the front door. Fifteen or so girls were there, and they all looked hot. A short blonde in the corner had on white cutoffs and a floral print bikini top from which she overflowed bountifully, a brunette with gorgeous legs had on a black lycra mini-dress that fit her like a second skin, a gorgeous black girl had on a white cat suit and leopard-print ankle boots. And in addition to looking great, it seemed to Sam that they were all completely confident, as if they could easily get up and sing in a Broadway show, no sweat. She hoped she was wrong.

"Sam!"

Sam heard Emma's voice calling, and she crossed the room to join her near the stage.

"You're so smart," Sam said, eyeing Emma's outfit appreciatively. Emma had chosen a lilac silk mini-shift, devoid of any ornamentation and impeccably cut. The perfect simplicity of it made Emma stand out from the crowd, sort of like whispering instead of shouting.

"This is really okay?" Emma asked Sam. "I had no idea what to wear."

"Believe me," Sam assured her, "everyone is making it up as they go along. Have you seen Diana De Bitch?"

Emma cocked her head to the left and rolled her eyes. Sam looked in the direction Emma had indicated. There was Diana, right next to Pres. She was dressed in tight black jeans and your basic Fruit of the Loom guy's white T-shirt. Evidently Diana had had the idea to dress casually, too. Her hand was draped over Pres's arm, and she was laughing at something he'd said.

"I'm going to go kill her," Sam said, her hands clenched into fists.

"She's not worth the jail time," Emma assured her.

"Hi, there," Carrie said, coming up beside them with her video camera poised. "You guys up for this?"

"Sure," Sam said, forcing herself to flash a self-confident smile at the camera.

"It's, like, so incredibly sexist!" a girl to their right said loudly to two other girls. It caught everyone's attention. Carrie aimed the video camera at her.

"You know what I mean," the girl continued earnestly to them. "Here we are, parading around like pieces of meat, hoping that these guys will pick us. I mean, it's demeaning!"

A slender girl with brown curls shrugged in response. "So if you feel that way then why are you here?"

"Because I'm a singer, that's why!" the first girl flared. "And you can't get a gig without peddling your tits and ass in the process!"

"So, start your own band, then," the slender girl said reasonably. "Then you won't have to put up with it."

"We all have to put up with it, anyway," the girl said with a sigh. "It's the culture."

The three girls walked away and Carrie put her camera down. "Wow, that was great," she said. "I'm glad I got it on tape."

"Do you think that girl is right?" Emma asked her friends.

"It's a dog-eat-dog world," Sam said philosophically. "Sometimes the best-looking dog gets the biscuits." She looked over at Diana, who was still chatting with Pres.

"But shouldn't it be about talent?" Emma asked.

"Oh, get over it, Em," Sam said, sounding sharper than she meant to. "You know very well that being good-looking is a huge asset in this world, no matter what you're trying to do."

"You don't need to snap at me," Emma answered.

"I'm sorry," Sam sighed. She was really upset over Diana and nervous about the audition, not mad at Emma.

"I'd say both things are true," Carrie mused. "The talent alone sometimes doesn't get a person a gig—although it should—but looks alone will never get it."

Sam raised her eyebrows. "If you believe that, then you don't know rock 'n' roll very well."

"Hi, everybody," Billy said from the stage. The conversations in the room came to a halt and everyone looked up at him expectantly. "Thanks a lot for coming back. Today we're going to be listening to you sing. We won't be listening for blend yet, just individual voices. So you can come up here one at a time and sing anything you want. Lisa over there—wave your hand,

Lisa"—a tall, thin young woman sitting at a piano waved her hand—"Lisa can play just about anything, so don't worry about it."

"But you didn't tell us to prepare a song!" one girl protested from the crowd.

"Yeah," someone else said. "I thought we'd just do backgrounds on one of the Flirts' tunes." There was some general noise of agreement from around the room.

"Well, you can do a Flirts' tune if you want," Billy said affably. "But we really need to hear you do more than background right now. I mean, you can sing 'God Bless America' if you want."

"Very sneaky," Sam said, leaning close to Emma. "He knows real singers won't get thrown by this—they've always got something prepared and they even know what key they sing it in."

"We put your names alphabetically, which means we start with . . ." Billy consulted a list. "Kimber Averly."

A short, plump girl with strawberry-blond hair and an air of confidence walked up onto the stage. She whispered something to Lisa, who nodded and started to play the opening chords to the Flirts' song "Hot Night." The girl threw her head back, brought the microphone close, and belted out the song.

"Wow, she's great," Emma breathed.

"No kidding," Sam muttered.

Carrie let her camera scan from Kimber Averly to faces in the crowd, then back to Kimber as she finished the song. Some people applauded, including Emma.

"She's really talented," Emma said. "I'm not even nervous anymore, because I know I'd never have a prayer against someone like her."

"Never say never," Sam advised, to herself as much as to Emma.

"Sam Bridges," Billy called from the stage.

"Good luck!" Emma whispered.

Carrie gave her the high-sign from behind the video camera, which followed Sam as she walked up onto the stage.

Sam spoke briefly with Lisa, and Lisa started playing Graham Perry's song "A Change Is Coming." Sam closed her eyes and swayed to the slow, insistent beat, then she opened her mouth and sang. Instead of belting it out and trying to compete with the girl with the strawberry-blond hair, Sam sang in a soft, breathy voice amplified by the microphone. Fortunately the song didn't have too wide of a range, and Sam gave it her all. After she sang the last note, she opened her eyes, shook her curls out of her face, and walked off the stage like a superstar.

"You were great!" Emma whispered, grabbing Sam's hand when she reached her.

"That was the most nervous I ever was in my life," Sam confessed in a shaky voice.

"Then you are a brilliant actress, Sam," Emma said. "No one would ever have known."

Sam snuck a look across the room at Pres where he sat taking notes with the rest of the band. He caught her eye and winked. She gave him a regal look and turned away. Her insides, however, were like jelly, and her stomach was cramped with anxiety. *Please let them like me*, Sam prayed silently. *Please*.

"Doreen Crasnowsky," Billy called out.

Doreen was a nervous wreck. She walked to the piano and Lisa made some suggestions. Doreen went to the microphone as "The Star-Spangled Banner" began to play.

"Bad choice," Sam murmured as Doreen started singing. "'The Star-Spangled Banner' is one of the toughest songs in the world to sing. It goes all over the place."

When Doreen got to the high part, she screeched into the microphone and her face turned scarlet with embarrassment. Still, she belted out the last lines for all she was worth, obviously hoping for the big finish. Her last note was noticeably flat, and she winced, and then shrugged as she walked off the stage.

"Emma Cresswell," Billy called.

Emma grabbed Sam's hand convulsively, and Sam gave her a reassuring squeeze. "I changed my mind," Emma said, "I am too nervous!"

"Go get 'em!" Sam urged, and, after consulting with Lisa, Emma walked to the microphone. She tapped the microphone lightly with her fingers, trying out the sound.

Oh, great, Sam thought to herself. *She's making it patently obvious that she's never used a mike before. Bad move.*

Emma took a deep breath as Lisa began to play. Then Emma's sweet, clear voice filled the air.

"Sometimes I feel like a motherless child.
Sometimes I feel like a motherless child.

Sometimes I feel like a motherless child. A long way from home."

My God, she has an absolutely beautiful voice, Sam thought to herself with surprise. She had known Emma's voice was pleasant, having heard her sing along to the radio often enough, but she'd had no idea that Emma could sing like this.

Emma finished the song and stepped back from the mike, then walked quickly off the stage. Carrie's video camera followed her every step of the way.

"Emma, that was incredible!" Sam cried when Emma reached her. "Whatever made you think of singing 'Motherless Child'?"

"I don't know, it just popped into my head!" Emma said, laughing with nervous relief that it was all over. "This Jamaican nanny I had when I was about four used to sing it to me whenever I cried. My mother fired her after a few months because she said the nanny didn't keep my dresses neat enough," she added.

"Diana De Witt!" Billy called, and the girls' attention was diverted back to the stage. Diana strode confidently up the steps, a cute long-haired guy trailing behind her.

"You can take a break, Lisa," she said. "I brought my own accompanist."

Lisa got up from the piano and the long-haired guy sat down. Diana walked over the microphone.

"This is a tune I wrote called 'Read My Lips,'" Diana said into the microphone in a throaty voice, then she nodded at the guy at the piano.

"Don't need words, baby
When I look at you.
Just read my lips
You'll know what I want to do . . ."

Diana swayed with the funky, bluesy music, running her hands through her hair and pouting her full lips seductively. Her eyes slid over the girls in the room and then the guys in the band, finally settling on Pres.

"Just read my lips
You'll know what I want to do."

Sam felt herself turning green as Diana finished singing and sashayed across the stage.

"She wasn't so great," Emma said.

"Wow, she's gonna get it for sure," a girl nearby said loudly. Everyone around her nodded in agreement.

Emma looked at Sam. "Her voice really isn't that special," Emma insisted.

But Sam hardly noticed what Emma was saying. She was too busy looking over at Pres. Diana was leaning over him in an intimate fashion. Suddenly Sam couldn't take it another moment. She was certain that not only was Diana going to get the gig that she wanted so badly, she was going to steal her boyfriend, too. Before she could think about how it would look, Sam turned and ran out of the club.

EIGHT

Sam drove straight back to the Jacobses', the radio blasting at full volume. She wanted to blast away all the anxieties that seemed to fill her life—the coolness with her parents, the search for her birth parents, the twins bickering, and now Diana De Witt deliberately trying to ruin her life. *How did everything get so complicated?*

When she pulled into the driveway she saw a Federal Express truck parked in front, and a young man at the front door.

"Can I help you?" Sam asked.

"Can you sign for this?" the man asked, thrusting a large envelope at Sam. It was addressed to her.

She hurriedly signed and opened the envelope on her way into the house. It was the adoption papers from her parents. A second, sealed enveloped was inside with a note on top.

Dear Sam,
   Your father and I are trying to understand how you feel. You know we're always here for you and we love you very much. Do what you think is best.
                                    Love,
                                    Mom

Do what I think is best, Sam repeated in her mind, turning the envelope over and over in her hands. Tears came to her eyes. Why was it so difficult in life to know what was best, anyway? She went upstairs and threw herself on her bed, falling into a deep, depressed sleep, the envelope still clutched in her hand.

"Sam?" Carrie's voice called to her from far away. "Sam?" It was more insistent now, forcing her out of her dream.

Sam awoke groggily and sat up. Emma and Carrie were standing in her doorway.

"We knocked and knocked downstairs, but

no one answered," Emma said. "You left the front door open."

"What time is it?" Sam asked. She looked over at the clock. Six o'clock. She'd been asleep for hours.

Suddenly what had happened at the Play Café came back to her.

"Oh, God," Sam groaned, her face in her hands. "I can't believe I just ran out of there with everyone watching me."

"If it makes you feel any better, everyone wasn't watching you," Carrie said, coming over to sit on the edge of Sam's bed. "The auditions went right on. Most people didn't even notice that you'd left."

"Did Pres?" Sam asked.

"I suppose so," Carrie admitted.

"Did Diana?" she continued.

"Well, yeah," Carrie said.

"I am totally screwed," Sam cried.

"I don't think so," Emma said. "I mean, there was no rule that you had to stay after you sang. Maybe you just looked confident enough to walk away without hearing all the competition."

"You think?" Sam asked doubtfully.

"Very possible," Emma said, nodding.

"How were the other girls?" Sam asked.

"A few were good, one Asian girl named Maia was really good, but most weren't anywhere near your league," Emma answered.

"Did you see Diana with Pres, practically throwing herself on him?" Sam said. "And he didn't look any too resistant. I don't know, I just lost it!"

"Hey, if Pres cares about you—and you know he does—" Carrie said, "it won't matter what Diana does."

"Oh, really?" Sam asked. "How about how she stole Kurt away from Emma last summer."

No one said anything for a moment.

"That was different," Emma finally said. "Kurt and I were having problems anyway."

"Look, Pres is responsible for himself," Carrie said firmly. "I mean, Diana can't 'steal' a guy from you. He's got a mind of his own."

"Yeah, a mind that sees this really great-looking babe who will obviously do *anything* to be one of his backup singers," Sam said bitterly. "And I do mean *anything*."

"Well, I still say you're underestimating Pres," Carrie argued. "You think he'd go after any good-looking girl who threw herself at him?"

"He's a guy, isn't he?" Sam said.

"Come on!" Carrie chided, nudging Sam's leg with her arm. "You're underestimating him in a big way."

"Maybe she is," Emma told Carrie, "but I can understand how threatened Sam feels. You might not feel so confident yourself if Diana were making a big play for Billy instead of Pres."

Carrie jumped up and paced around the room. "Come on, you guys! It isn't like that!"

Sam pushed her hair out of her eyes. "I'll tell you what's making me really, really crazy—and don't try to tell me this doesn't make a difference, Carrie," Sam said. "I'm not sleeping with Pres. We don't even have a commitment that we won't see other people, or anything like that. And Diana makes it perfectly clear what she's after. So I ask you, why shouldn't he go along with it?"

Neither Carrie nor Emma had a quick answer for that one.

"Just don't go to bed with him because you're afraid she will," Carrie said, sliding down the wall to sit on the floor. "I mean, that shouldn't be the reason."

"I know that," Sam sighed, "but I've got to admit, it's tempting."

"Maybe Pres wouldn't sleep with Diana even if he's physically attracted to her, because basically she's an obnoxious bitch," Emma offered.

"Maybe," Sam said dubiously. "But in my experience with guys, when the old lust antenna goes up, their minds go completely blank." She gestured with her hand, and accidentally knocked to the floor the envelope from her parents. Carrie picked it up and handed it to her, glancing at the return address.

"From home?" Carrie asked.

Sam nodded, staring down at the envelope she still hadn't opened. "I called and told my mother about looking for my biological parents," Sam said.

"So what did she say?" Emma asked.

"She said she and my father are against it," Sam said bitterly, "but they sent me all the information they have, anyway. She said it has to be my choice."

"Well, that's great!" Carrie exclaimed. "That's just what you wanted!"

"I know," Sam acknowledged, staring down at the envelope. "So why do I feel so crappy, then?"

"Aren't you going to open it?" Emma asked gently.

Sam didn't say anything for a minute. "You know, secrets suck," she finally said, lifting her head to look at Emma. "My life will never be the same because my parents lied to me all those years."

Carrie put her hand on Sam's arm, and Sam turned to look at her. "Well, maybe now the truth can set you free."

Sam felt as if she could hear the beating of her own heart. "You're right," she finally whispered. She put her fingernail under the edge of the envelope to rip it open, just as she heard the door bang open downstairs.

"He was not talking to you, you grease-faced oinker!" one of the twins screamed. "He was talking to me!"

"Oh, yeah?" the other twin taunted. "Then why did he say I had great long hair, answer me that? You have short hair and you look like a boy!"

"Girls, we had such a lovely day together," Mr. Jacobs cut in.

"God, is it always like this?" Carrie asked Sam.

"Sometimes it's worse," Sam sighed.

"Sam?" Mr. Jacobs yelled upstairs.

"Right here!" Sam called, walking into the hall.

"Could you get a barbecue started out on the patio?"

"Sure," Sam called down.

"I am not eating meat!" one of the twins yelled. "It's disgusting."

"Gee, I love my job," Sam said sarcastically, walking back over to her bed.

"Have they tried family counseling or something?" Carrie asked.

"What family counselor would put up with them?" Sam asked. She picked up the envelope again, and then set it down on her dresser. "I guess I'll have to deal with this later."

"Well, I guess we should go," Emma said, getting up. "You're okay?"

"Basically," Sam said with a shrug. "When did the Flirts say they'd let us know who made it into the finals."

"The list will be posted tomorrow morning about ten," Carrie said, hoisting her shoulder bag up on her arm. "I'm going to try to video the girls' reaction when they see the list."

"Do me a favor," Sam said. "Turn the camera off when I get there, just in case it's bad news."

"Stop worrying so much," Emma said. "You were terrific!"

"Well, maybe so," Sam acknowledged, "but that was before I bolted like a total fool."

Emma and Carrie hugged Sam and left. Sam put the envelope in her top drawer, amid the pocket change, letters, and lipstick tubes. *It's kept this long*, she thought. *It'll keep a little longer.* But she couldn't quite figure out why she was so afraid of looking at what was inside.

"Turn the tape off, Carrie," Sam said. "I mean it."

It was the next morning and Sam had just walked into the Play Café to see if her name was on the list of finalists. She'd slept badly the night before, and a dull headache was pounding behind her eyes. No amount of makeup or hair spray helped promote a feeling of self-confidence. And a little voice in her head kept saying, *Pres wasn't even concerned enough to call you. If he cared about you, and certainly if you made it to the finals, he would have called to see why you ran out.* But there had been no phone call, no southern cutie leaning against a motorcycle in her driveway, no nothing.

Carrie obliged and put down the video camera. "Listen, Sam, you don't have to—" Carrie began.

"Oh, excuse me," Diana said as she pushed open the door to the club and practically ran into Sam. Then she realized to whom she was apologizing. "Well, well," she said, a nasty grin spreading across her face. "Look who's here. You know, Sam, I had no idea that you could run as fast as I saw you run yesterday. But then, I guess those stork legs of yours should come in handy for something."

Sam put her hands on her hips and eyed Diana frostily. "Stork legs?" she repeated. "Diana, kids called me that in junior high. You're slipping."

Diana laughed. "I'd love to stay and trade wittier insults but I have to go look at my name on the list over there."

"What makes you so sure you're on it?" Sam asked.

"Pres told me, that's why," Diana said innocently.

Sam felt as if a knife were twisting in her heart. No words would come to her lips, and Diana just smiled serenely and walked away.

"He told her and not me?" Sam whispered to Carrie, tears filling her eyes. "That means she got it and I didn't," she said, gulping hard. "That means she got *him* and I didn't!"

"But you *did* make the finals, that's what I was trying to tell you when you came in!" Carrie exclaimed.

"I did?" Sam said, clutching Carrie's arm.

"Go look!"

Sam ran across the room to the bulletin board. She stepped around Diana and three disappointed-looking girls, one of whom was actually crying. The list had only five names on it. It read:

> KIMBER AVERLY
> SAM BRIDGES
> EMMA CRESSWELL
> DIANA DE WITT
> MAIA JONG

117

Diana turned to look at Sam. "Well, doesn't this get juicy," she murmured.

"Hey, Diana, I'm the one with professional experience," Sam reminded her, trying to act as if she weren't surprised to see her name on the list at all.

"Yeah, I heard that you were a pro," Diana said with a nod. "But then who can blame a poor girl like you for making money on her back," she added.

"If I did do that, which I don't," Sam shot back, "I'd be a hell of a lot smarter than you, because you give it away."

"Maybe I do and maybe I don't," Diana purred, not stung in the least. She ran her hand through her curls and smiled at Sam, then turned to leave. "Oh, by the way," she said, turning back to Sam as if she forgotten something. "Did I mention that Pres is a great kisser?" Then she walked out of the club.

Emma came in just as Diana was leaving. "So glad I missed the wicked witch," Emma said, walking over to the bulletin board.

"She just told me what a great kisser Pres is," Sam said dully.

"Just because she said it doesn't mean she really knows," Emma pointed out, scanning the list quickly. "Sam, my name is here!" she cried out. "I can't believe it! My name is really here!"

"Congrats to you both," Carrie said. "Now can I turn on the camera?"

"Sure!" Emma cried happily. "You can catch me as I walk ten feet off the ground!"

Carrie hoisted the camera and turned it on Emma's grinning face.

"I made the finals!" Emma told the camera.

Carrie laughed. "This is not a home movie!" she protested. "You're supposed to pretend the camera isn't there."

"Oh, okay," Emma said. She turned to Sam and shook her by the shoulders, which meant reaching up about six inches. "We made the finals!" she yelled happily.

"Do you think she really kissed him?" Sam asked anxiously. She was so upset about what Diana had said that she didn't even notice that Carrie was taping.

"I'm telling you, she's trying to psych you out," Emma insisted. "And it's working!"

"But she said he told her she was a finalist," Sam insisted. "I sure didn't get any phone calls from him!"

"She could easily have lied about that, too," Emma assured Sam.

Sam sighed and rubbed her tired eyes. "I have to get back to work."

"You could always call Pres and ask him what's going on," Emma suggested gently.

Sam shook her head no. "I can't do that," she said softly. "Let's face it. I'm a huge flirt. I don't have any right to tell him he can't go out with Diana." She pulled her car keys out of her purse. "See you guys later," she said, walking forlornly toward the door.

"Hey, Sam," Emma called to her. "What did you decide to do about the papers from your parents?"

"I overnighted them to Family Finders before I came here," Sam said.

"So what did the papers say?" Emma asked.

"I didn't read them," Sam admitted. "I didn't open the envelope." She stared at her car keys a moment. "I got scared," she whispered.

"It's okay, Sam," Emma said, putting her hand on Sam's arm. "It's really okay."

Sam attempted a smile, but it wavered on her lips. "Sometimes I don't understand myself at all," she admitted.

"Join the club," Emma said ruefully.

Carrie had put the camera down, and she walked over to Emma and Sam. "For whatever it's worth," she told Sam, "I think you're the greatest."

"Me, too," Emma said firmly.

Sam looked at Emma's and Carrie's solemn faces. They looked so serious, she just had to laugh. "Personally, I think all three of us are probably certifiable."

"Could be," Emma agreed. "Listen, the finals are tomorrow night. Do you think you and I could work on harmony parts later tonight? I haven't had to sing harmonies since I was in a madrigal group at boarding school."

"Sure," Sam said. "Come over about eight. The monsters are going to the movies—so much for being grounded," she added ironically. "But listen, harmony singing is not my long suit."

"So we'll help each other," Emma said. "We only have to beat out two girls on that list, then we're in!"

"Wow, what an attitude change!" Carrie laughed.

"I just never, ever in my wildest dreams thought I'd get this far," Emma explained.

121

"So now I think anything might be possible!"

"Hey, you guys are going to the clambake tomorrow, aren't you?" Carrie said.

"I am," Emma answered. "The whole Hewitt family is going. Katie has been chattering about it for days."

"From what I hear all the summer people will be there," Carrie said. "Claudia was on the committee. The Chamber of Commerce wants it to become an annual event."

"Mr. Jacobs is bringing the monsters—I guess that doesn't count against being grounded, either," Sam said, shaking her head. "Anyway, I can come solo, and it will take my mind off the finals."

"You're going to do great, both of you," Carrie said. "I really think you can beat out the competition."

"Well, as long as we beat out Diana De Witt," Sam said with a sigh, "I, for one, will live happily ever after."

Sam waved good-bye and walked out to the car, a little prayer continuing in her mind. *One other thing*, she prayed. *Please let me beat Diana out for Pres, too. Oh, yeah. And one more thing. Please let me find my birth mother, and—this wish is a two-parter—please have her be as incredible as I imagine she will be. This is Sam, did you get all that?*

As she slid into the driver's seat, she laughed out loud at herself. *Just who am I supposed to be praying to? I'm the one who always insists I don't even believe in God.* But right at that moment, she wished she could believe in something—in anything—that was bigger than her small, totally confused self.

NINE

I can't believe I'm doing this, Sam thought to herself ruefully as she sat on the top step of the stairway leading to Graham Perry Templeton's basement. *It's not enough that I have to go through the drill of auditioning to sing backup to the Flirts, but now I'm chaperoning the monsters for their first rehearsal as backup singers to Lord Whitehead and the Zitmen!*

Sitting on the steps, Sam recalled that Ian Templeton, son of rock superstar Graham Perry, had formed a band at his boarding school that played something they called "industrial music." He had recently resurrected his band, with new musicians, on the island. Carrie had described industrial music as consisting of banging on the insides of old washing machines and other appliances, while singing along to a background of taped popular music. *And this is the band that Becky and Allie are going to join?* It was hard to imagine.

Sam moved down a few steps and looked down at an almost unbelievable scene. The basement was jam-packed with all sorts of hulked-out appliances and broken-down factory equipment—and in and among the flotsam were four teenage boys, including Ian, and Becky and Allie. Ian was standing on an overturned milk crate, calling for attention. *Oh, good grief,* Sam thought, trying to hold back a chuckle. *He's about to make a speech.*

"Fellow artists," Ian said in an affected English accent. "Who am I?"

"Lord Whitehead!" one of the boys shouted.

"And who are you?" Ian queried haughtily. Sam couldn't take it. She buried her face in her hands to muffle her laughter.

"We are the Zitmen!" all three boys yelled back.

"Hey! Excuuuuuuse me!" said Becky, marching right up to Ian. She was just about as tall as he, even though he was perched on the milk crate.

126

"Yes, Zit?" Ian looked down his nose at Becky imperiously.

"You got girls in the band, now, Ian," Becky said, getting right in Ian's face. "We can't be the Zit*men* anymore."

"In the future, address me as Lord, Zit," Ian said. Becky rolled her eyes. Then there was dead silence in the room, except for Sam's chuckling, as Ian seemed to reach a decision.

"Yes, yes, quite right," he said, still talking as if he were a member of the British Parliament. "I will remain Lord Whitehead, but you are no longer the Zitmen."

Sam could hear one boy whisper loudly to another, "I would never put up with this crap if his dad weren't Graham Perry." The second boy nodded in agreement.

"From this moment on, this band shall be known as Lord Whitehead and the Zit *People*," Ian pronounced, banging on the milk crate with his foot for emphasis. "Not the Zits, but the Zit People." For a moment Ian lost his haughty look. He turned to Becky. "Uh, is that okay?"

Becky looked over at Allie, who shrugged her shoulders. "Okay," Becky said to Ian, "but if people throw tubes of Clearasil at us on stage, I'm quitting."

"Me, too," Allie said.

"Okay," Ian intoned. "Places, everyone."

The kids all jumped to their positions. Sam looked on as the three other boys grabbed batons, a crowbar, and what looked like a broken hockey stick, and arranged themselves behind their industrial instruments. Becky and Allie, meanwhile, sidled up to a single microphone somewhat behind where Ian stood. Ian's mike was located front and center, right near a big cassette recorder.

"This song is going to be the Zit People's signature number, and I'm sure you all listened to your rehearsal cassettes," Ian announced as the band fidgeted in their places. "It's a rock classic." Ian reached down and flipped the music on. The raspy sound of a male voice filled the room.

"Sometimes I feel like a motherless child
Sometimes I feel like a motherless child
Sometimes I feel like a motherless child
Such a long, long, long way from home.
Freedom, yeah freedom . . ."

128

Sam sat bolt upright. *That's Emma's audition song,* she thought to herself. *And I recognize the voice. It's Richie Havens's version, from the Woodstock soundtrack album. My dad sometimes plays that when he's cleaning out the garage!*

At the first chorus of "Freedom," the band broke into its characteristic cacophony of noise. The Zit People banged and clanked on their appliances, Ian started wailing "Freedom!" at the top of his lungs, and the monsters sang the words "I'm a child" over and over again, leaning seductively into their mike the way they'd seen it done on MTV.

Sam's jaw dropped. She was prepared for it to be bad, but not this bad. *Diana De Witt should be sentenced to sing backup for this group,* she thought.

Mercifully the song ended quickly. Just as the sound stopped, Sam heard the basement door open. Carrie, who had been out grocery shopping for the clambake, stepped inside.

"How are they doing?" Carrie asked Sam, sitting down beside her.

Sam made sure Ian was busy giving instructions to his band before she spoke. "It's . . . unbelievable," Sam said.

Carrie winced. "That bad, huh?"

"Worse," Sam answered honestly. "And Ian is acting mondo-bizarro—ordering everyone around in this affected English accent," Sam said. "What happened to the sweet kid I know and love?"

"The sweet kid is going through what is commonly called 'a stage,'" Carrie said ruefully.

"Oh, yeah, a stage." Sam nodded. "The monsters are in a permanent 'stage.'"

"Hey, Ian," Carrie called across the room. "Don't forget the clambake. Your mom already went over there with Chloe. We've got to be at the beach in an hour."

"No way," Ian said firmly. "I'm in the middle of practice here. I'll meet you there."

"No you won't," Carrie said reasonably. "I told your parents I'd drive you over, so that's what I'm going to do."

Sam saw Ian roll his eyes with exasperation. "Okay, okay," he finally said. "Zit People," he called to his band, "back to work!"

Sam and Carrie went upstairs, and made it as far as the Templetons' den before they both collapsed in gales of laughter.

"Zit People??" Sam could barely get the

words out. "Watch out, Flirts, watch out, Springsteen, you've got comp!"

"Stranger things have happened," Carrie said. "But I can't say I know what."

Two hours later, Sam, Carrie, and Emma were sitting on a blanket at the beach. It was late in the afternoon, and their part of the beach was filled with dozens of families who summered on the island.

The Hewitts were camped out near one of the dunes. The Templetons were sitting with some friends near the water's edge. And Mr. Jacobs was near the clambake itself, and looked as though he was flirting with two women simultaneously. The twins, per usual, were flirting outrageously with every cute guy they could find.

"This is way cool," Sam said, pulling her sunglasses out of her bag. "I can see how it could become an annual event."

"Yep, it's postcard perfect, all right," Carrie agreed. "But you notice the poor people who live on the island aren't sunning and funning at this little party," she pointed out.

"Please," Sam begged. "No politics now. It interferes with my appetite." She smacked her lips scrumptiously. "Can't say

I've ever been to a New England clambake before, but I like it, I like it!"

Emma laughed. "It's because you can get enough to eat for a change."

"No kidding," Sam replied, biting into a third ear of roasted corn. "I won't have to eat again until maybe eight o'clock this evening."

The food was amazing. Earlier in the day, some of the families had dug a huge pit and built a fire in the bottom of it. When the fire burned down to just coals, they filled the pit with wrapped lobsters, clams, mussels, scallops, baking potatoes, and ears of corn, all in different layers. Then they covered the top of the pit, and let all the food bake. When it came time to eat, the pit was unearthed, and the delicious smelling seafood taken out, perfectly done.

"Looks like a scene from a Norman Rockwell painting," Emma mused, gazing around at the people eating. One group had finished dinner and had started a spirited game of beach volleyball. Another group was flying big colorful kites out over the dunes.

"Hey, look who's coming this way!" Emma said, pointing toward the parking area. "It's Darcy and Molly!"

"Over here!" Emma called out to them.

Darcy was a tall, lovely girl their age with stunning long black hair. She had grown up in Bangor, Maine, on what she referred to as "the wrong side of the tracks." Darcy was athletic and anything but petite, and could take care of herself in almost any situation.

At the moment, she was carrying sixteen-year-old Molly Mason across the sand with her without missing a step. Molly had fair skin and chestnut-colored curls, and when she wasn't scowling and in one of her moods, Sam reflected, she was very pretty. Molly had been in a car accident a year earlier, and ever since had been confined to a wheel-chair.

Darcy's job was to take care of Molly, although she readily admitted that she thought of her more as a friend than as her work.

"I guess Darcy can't get Molly's wheel-chair through the sand," Sam murmured, watching the two girls approach.

"Hi, there!" Darcy said, setting Molly down on the colorful blanket Carrie had spread out. "Long time no see and all that!"

"Great to see you guys!" Carrie said.

"I bet you're surprised to see me," Molly said with a small grin.

That's true, Sam thought to herself. As far as she knew getting Molly to go out in public was like pulling teeth. Darcy had told them that Molly couldn't stand to have people stare at her.

"It was the lure of the baked clams that did it," Darcy said. "I kept describing how good the food would be, and Molly couldn't resist."

"A woman after my own heart." Sam laughed, handing Molly a paper plate. "Go for it!"

"Hey, I went to the Play Café the other day and I saw two familiar names on the finalist list for the Flirts' audition," Darcy said, taking an ear of corn.

"The Flirts are great," Molly said. "Congrats."

"Thanks, but they didn't pick the backups yet," Sam pointed out.

"Oh, yes they did," Darcy said cheerfully, biting into her corn.

"No they didn't," Sam insisted. "We have the finals tonight and . . ." Then she stopped, remembering something about Darcy. Darcy was psychic. Not all the time, which Darcy found maddening because she had no control over it. Still, she seemed awfully sure about what she was saying.

"Wait a second," Sam said slowly. "Is this one of those psychic flashes of yours?"

Darcy grinned. "Let's just say that while it isn't a sure thing, you two would have to howl like banshees at the final audition tonight to wreck it."

Sam looked over at Emma. "Did you hear that?" she asked, grabbing Emma's arm.

"That's . . . that's just incredible!" Emma exclaimed.

"So you're saying we could still blow it, but we've got a really good shot?" Sam asked.

Darcy nodded. "I had a dream where you and Emma were surrounded by a bright light, and people were applauding."

"This is so cool," Sam said, hugging her knees to her chest.

"Of course, the bright light could be a police lineup, and some dire enemy could be applauding because they hate you so much," Molly said jokingly.

"Very funny," Darcy said with a chuckle.

"Dire enemy," Sam said, frowning. "That's Diana De Witt." She clutched Darcy's arm.

"Is she going to be the third person? I have to know!"

"Yo, Sam, chill!" Darcy laughed. "Molly was only kidding. And I didn't get any kind of vibes about Diana De Witt at all."

"That's because she's like a vampire," Carrie said, wiggling her eyebrows. "She casts no shadow, you can't dream about her, and she always goes for the jugular."

"The only person I know who probably dreams about her is Pres," Sam said glumly, licking some butter off her fingers.

"Are the Flirts coming to the clambake?" Emma asked.

"Billy said they were coming over later," Carrie said.

"I wish Kurt could be here," Emma sighed. "He's working, as usual."

"Hi, ladies!" All five girls turned to see Howie Lawrence standing next to their blanket in a pair of cutoffs and a blue T-shirt, and spinning a Frisbee in his right hand.

He must have seen that Billy wasn't with Carrie, so he moved in for the kill! Sam thought to herself, smiling.

"Hi, Howie," Emma spoke up first. "Having a good time?"

"Great," Howie said. "Hi, I'm Howie Lawrence," he said to Darcy and Molly.

Emma quickly introduced them. Sam noticed his eyes flick over Molly with interest.

"Just wanted to know if you ladies wanted to see me embarrass Butchie in Frisbee."

"Say what?" Sam asked skeptically. The previous summer, Butchie, a well-known local bully, had whipped Howie at the Play Café's pool table, and then tried to intimidate him into paying even more than their bet.

"Yup," Howie continued. "Butchie saw me with the Frisbee and challenged me to a fifty-dollar bet that he could throw it farther than I could. Best of three tries."

He's about to lose again, Sam thought. *I've seen Butchie with a Frisbee on the beach, and he is good!*

"Why not?" Carrie said. "Let's go," she said to her friends.

They all followed Howie to a less crowded area of the beach. Butchie was already waiting with his friends, juggling a couple of Frisbees.

"Hey, Big Red!" Butchie said when he spied Sam. "What brings you to my side of the beach?"

"I'm here to watch Howie embarrass you," Sam responded cheerfully.

"Ha!" Butchie said, continuing to juggle the Frisbees.

"Shall we begin?" Howie asked.

Whoa, he is mondo-confident for someone who's about to get his butt kicked, Sam thought.

"Ante up first," Butchie said, holding out a fifty-dollar bill. "Let Big Red hold the money."

Sam took Butchie's fifty, and then one from Howie.

"Okay, here's the rules," Howie said. He drew a line in the sand. "You have to throw from behind this line. We alternate throws. The person whose Frisbee goes farthest wins, okay? You go first." He motioned to Butchie to start. Butchie was smirking.

Obviously he thinks this will be like taking candy from a baby, Sam thought. *He's twice Howie's size!* She watched as Butchie selected one of his Frisbees, paced off several steps behind the line drawn in the sand, ran forward, and let fly.

Wow! What a throw! Butchie's first toss went for what seemed like forever.

"My turn," Howie said, completely undaunted. He took a Frisbee, walked back, and flipped his wrist. It was a good toss, but it was at least twenty yards shorter than his competitor's.

The next round went exactly the same way.

"One round left," Butchie said to Howie maliciously. "If you want to quit now, I'll halve the bet just to prove to Big Red I'm a good guy—if she'll kiss me!" He smiled leeringly at Sam.

What a wanker, Sam thought.

"No, I don't think so," Howie said thoughtfully. "Why don't we double it instead?"

Butchie hit his ear as if he were hearing things. "Say what?" he said.

"Double the bet, can't you understand English?" Howie said, smiling. "Two times fifty is one hundred."

Sam couldn't believe her ears. *Howie's going to lose his money again.* She looked at her friends. They were both shaking their heads. She looked over at Butchie, who was carefully giving Howie the once-over, as if wondering whether he was about to be hustled. Then Sam saw Butchie burst into a big grin.

"Okay, sucker," Butchie said. "It's your money. I know you can afford it."

"Ante up!" Howie said, and Sam took an additional fifty dollars from both guys. Then Butchie took a Frisbee, backed off, and let fly with a toss that was his best yet. Howie applauded politely.

"Nice throw, Butchie. Now, watch this," he said, taking his own Frisbee and backing off.

Sam watched, fascinated, as Howie grasped the Frisbee. *He's holding it backward*, she thought. Howie waited for a good gust of wind, and then whirled around and around like a discus thrower at the Olympics before finally hurling it down the beach.

His throw outdistanced Butchie's best by ten yards. Butchie's jaw dropped. Sam and the girls cheered wildly.

"Overhand wrist flip, Butchie, learned it at college," Howie said mildly. "Maybe you ought to think about continuing your education."

"Maybe you ought to get your skinny butt out of here," Butchie growled, "before I kick it all over Maine. Nobody hustles me and gets away with it."

Sam couldn't help herself, even though

she had vowed to never to say another word to Butchie. "He just did," she said to him and triumphantly handed the two-hundred-dollar ante to Howie.

The girls laughed all the way back to their beach blanket. Sam's mind wandered back to the auditions, and her problems with Pres. *Where is he, anyway?* she thought as she walked. *According to Carrie, he should have been here already.*

"Hey, there's Pres!" Carrie pointed to Pres taking his helmet off next to his motorcycle. Sam's eyes lit on another person, female, removing her helmet and shaking out her curls.

Oh, my God, it's Diana, Sam realized. *Pres came here with Diana.*

"Now, don't jump to conclusions," Emma cautioned.

"Say, Darcy," Sam asked in a steely voice. "Are you sure you didn't have a dream about a certain redhead who murders a certain brunette whose initials are D.D.?"

"Can't say that I did," Darcy admitted.

"Too bad," Sam said, "because it's just about to come true."

TEN

"There she is," Sam hissed to Emma that evening at the Play Café. Sam and Emma had arrived for the final round of auditions, and Diana was just breezing through the door. "I should have punched her lights out this afternoon when I had the chance. You shouldn't have stopped me."

"You could be worrying about nothing, which is just what I told you before," Emma reminded her. "After all, you took off this afternoon before you knew what was really going on."

"It was either that or murder," Sam said, watching Diana out of the side of her eyes.

"Hi, girls," Diana said, walking boldly over to them. "Have fun at the clambake? Pres and I did."

Sam's hands clenched and unclenched at her sides. She tried to keep her voice steady. "Oh, Diana, I'm sure you had 'fun' with any number of guys this afternoon," Sam said. "How could one possibly be enough for you?"

Diana looked over at Pres, who was across the room going through some sheet music. "Depends on who the one is," Diana replied. She looked from Sam to Emma and back to Sam again. "You two both seem to have a real problem holding on to your boyfriends. Too bad," she crooned, and walked away.

"God, wasn't it enough that she managed to snare Kurt from you last summer?" Sam seethed to Emma. "Does she have to take Pres, too?"

"That comment is not worthy of you," Carrie said as she came up beside her two friends. "You act like she has all this power and you're powerless."

"I can't believe how much I let her get to me," Sam moaned. "I don't even like the me I become around her!"

"Not to mention that you haven't really talked to Pres for days," Carrie pointed out, pushing her hair behind an ear. "You don't even know what the real deal is."

"Okay," Sam resolved, folding her arms firmly, "as of this minute I am changing my attitude. Screw Pres and Diana and all this petty crap. I'm going to concentrate on giving the audition of my life tonight."

"Me, too," Emma agreed. "If Darcy's prediction was right, we're about to become professional backup singers!"

"Okay, ladies, gather 'round the piano, please," Billy said. The five girls came up on stage. Carrie went to get her video camera.

"First I want to thank all of you for going through this," Billy said, fiddling with the diamond stud in his ear. "I know it's been a pain. I want to tell you all how talented we think you are."

From the table near the stage Pres and the rest of the guys in the band nodded in agreement. Sam could feel Pres looking in her direction, but she refused to make eye contact with him. She kept her eyes firmly focused on Billy.

"Unfortunately," Billy continued, "we can only choose three backup singers. So we're going to listen to blends on harmony lines,

and that's how we'll make the final decision."
He pulled out a lead sheet and set it on the
piano. "This is a new tune that Pres wrote
called 'Maybe.' The backup vocals will come
in on three-part harmonies on the chorus. It
goes:

"Maybe we're together
Maybe we're apart.
Maybe I can't see what's in your heart.
Maybe you've got feelings
Or maybe you're too tough
But if you want to take a chance, maybe it's
   love."

"Great tune," Maia, the Asian girl, said as
soon as Billy finished singing and playing
the chorus.

*Yeah. And maybe he wrote "Maybe" for
Diana,* Sam thought miserably to herself.
No. I'm not going to think about that now.

"If you gather around the sheet music, I'll
go over the harmony lines," Billy said.

The girls all obliged. Sam noticed that
Kimber, the strawberry-blonde with the big
belt voice, let her hand trail across Billy's
shoulders as she leaned forward to look at
the sheet music. Sam looked over at Carrie

146

to see if she'd caught the move, but she couldn't see Carrie's face behind the video camera.

"Okay, that's it," Billy said when he'd finished. "Any problems?"

"Could you go over the soprano part of the last line again, please?" Emma asked in a small voice.

"Sure," Billy said, and he played the line again.

"Thanks." Emma nodded. "I think I've got it."

"Anyone else?" Billy asked.

Sam desperately wanted to ask to hear both the low and the high parts again. She had a terrible time retaining the harmony lines even after she thought she knew them—she'd had the same problem at Disney World. When she worked extra hard to learn a vocal part, though, she found she could keep right up with the singers to whom it came more quickly. Just as she had worked up her nerve to ask Billy to play the harmonies again, Maia said with a shrug, "It's a real straightforward one-three-five harmony. Piece of cake."

"Okay, we're going to do harmony mix-and-match here," Billy said, looking around

147

at the girls contemplatively. "How about we start with Diana on alto, Sam on melody, and Maia on soprano."

There is a God! Sam exalted silently. *Billy put me on melody!*

Diana, Sam, and Maia stood together as Billy played the final line of the verse leading into the chorus. All three girls came in at the same time and sang. Sam was too busy trying to remember the melody line to notice how either Maia or Diana were doing. It seemed to her that someone was flat at some point, but she couldn't pick out who it was— for all she knew, it was her!

"Great," Billy said. "Now how about Kimber on alto, Emma on melody, and Maia on soprano again."

Maia is singing again, Sam thought. *He must really like her voice.* Now that she wasn't singing, Sam listened critically to the three voices. Emma sounded great! Kimber sang louder, which didn't really balance since Emma was on the melody line. And this time she identified Maia as the one who was a little flat.

Billy mixed the voices around again and again, and for some reason Sam could only assume was the greatest luck in the world, every time she sang, she sang melody. Emma got switched from soprano to melody to soprano again. After more than an hour of this, Billy went over to talk with the rest of the band.

"What do you think they're saying?" Emma whispered to Sam.

"They probably decided a long time ago about us and now they're trying to figure out where to go for burgers," Sam joked.

Finally Billy walked back over to them. "Okay, it looks like we're done." He looked at his watch. "I promised the owner I'd turn his club back over to him, anyway," Billy said with a grin.

"When will we find out something?" Maia asked.

"Tonight," Billy said. "After everything you've been through I don't think you should have to lose any sleep wondering if you made it or not."

"We'll call ya'll," Pres drawled, walking over to the group, "whether you made it or not. And we really do want to thank you again for all the time you've put into this."

"When's the first gig?" Diana asked as she picked up her purse from the table.

"Here at the Play Café next weekend,"

Billy said. "It's payback for using the club for all these auditions."

"Cool," Maia said. She flung her arms around Billy's neck and hugged him sexily, then pulled away so she could look at him, her arms still locked around his neck. "This was really fun, Billy," she said softly.

"Thanks again, everyone," Billy said, gently extricating himself from Maia's arms.

Diana walked over to Pres and hugged him the same way that Maia had hugged Billy. "It was about as much fun as you can have standing up," she said, gazing at him seductively.

"You were terrific," Pres told her. He looked over at Sam.

"Come on, Emma, we're out of here," Sam said, briskly walking toward the door.

"Hey, Sam . . . " Pres called to her.

But Sam just ignored him and headed for the door.

"Why didn't you see what he wanted?" Emma asked Sam when they hit the sidewalk.

"Because I have better things to do with my time than be humiliated by that lowlife," Sam snapped. "Did you see him with her? Did you?"

"As far as I could see she was doing everything, and he was just standing there," Emma said mildly.

"Then what was that 'you were terrific' comment to her," Sam demanded.

"He was referring to her voice," Emma pointed out.

"Please," Sam scoffed. "I have a brain in my head." She pulled her car keys out of her bag. "Call me as soon as you hear anything, okay?"

"Ditto," Emma said.

"Oh, I'm glad I caught you two," Carrie said, coming out of the club. "They're about to open the doors for business. Do you want to stay and get something to eat?"

"I'm too nervous," Emma admitted, putting her hand gracefully over her stomach.

"And I can't stand to look at Diana and Pres together another minute," Sam said. "It makes me sick."

Just at that minute Diana came out of the club, Pres right behind her.

"Sam!" Pres said when he saw her. "I'm glad I caught you. I thought maybe we could—"

"You didn't catch me," Sam interrupted. "I'm just leaving. I've got a date," she added fatuously. *Now why did I say that,* Sam asked herself. *I sound like a total idiot.*

"Oh, well then," Diana said smoothly, taking Pres's arm, "there's nothing to stop us from going for a ride on your bike, is there?"

"Hey, knock yourself out," Sam said before she could hear Pres's answer. "I'm gone." Sam turned on her heel and walked briskly to the parking lot.

When she got home she heard voices coming from the den.

"Hi, Sam," Mr. Jacobs said when he saw her. "This is Tanya Connors. Tanya, this is Sam Bridges, our au pair."

Mr. Jacobs sat on the couch, his arm around one of the women Sam had seen him flirting with at the clambake. Tanya had high cheekbones, a great tan, and sleek blond hair pulled back into a French braid. She wore a pair of well-cut linen pants and a summer sweater that Sam reckoned cost more than her entire wardrobe.

"Pleased ta meet cha," Tanya said in a heavy New York accent.

Sam bit her lips to keep from laughing. The woman's regal exterior was completely blown as soon as she opened her mouth.

"Yeah, same here," Sam managed. "Are

the twins in bed already?" she asked Mr. Jacobs.

He nodded. "They turned in early. They're sleeping like little angels," he added with a fond paternal smile.

Yeah, right, Sam thought.

"Those girls are the cutest!" Tanya exclaimed nasally. "Swear to God, the cutest!"

Mr. Jacobs hugged her shoulder in obvious agreement.

"Aren't they, though?" Sam said. "Well, I'll be going upstairs now. Oh, I'm expecting a phone call—I don't think it'll come too late," Sam added.

"Cool," Dan said, turning back to Tanya.

Cool? Sam repeated to herself as she walked upstairs. *I think I liked Mr. Jacobs better before he became a stud muffin. On the other hand, his love life is a lot better than mine.*

Just as Sam was about to throw herself on her bed, the phone rang. She ran to grab it.

"Jacobs residence," she said.

"Hi, it's me!" Emma's voice chirped happily.

"Did you hear something already?" Sam asked, clutching the phone hard.

"Yes, didn't you?" Emma asked, confusion in her voice.

"No," Sam admitted, gulping hard. "So . . . what's the news?"

"I got it!" Emma screamed. "It's unbelievable, but it's true!"

"Well, congratulations," Sam managed.

"But I was sure Billy already called you," Emma said.

"Nobody's called me," Sam told her. "Did Billy . . . did he say who else they hired?"

"He wouldn't tell me," Emma allowed, "but I just assumed . . ."

"Well, I haven't heard squat," Sam said in a flat voice.

"But Pres said they were going to call everyone, so I'm sure you'll get a call," Emma mused. "Listen, you definitely made it. There's no way you didn't make it!"

"Who knows," Sam sighed. At that moment she didn't feel confident at all. Even Darcy's prediction that both she and Emma would get hired seemed meaningless.

"I was just so sure they'd call you first," Emma said. "It never occurred to me that . . ."

Sam heard a short beep on the phone.

"Hold on, Emma, that's the call waiting," Sam said.

She pushed the button down on the phone.

"Hello?"

"Hi, Sam. It's Billy."

"Hi" was all Sam could get out of her mouth.

"I really want to thank you for auditioning for us," Billy began.

Oh, no, Sam thought wildly. *It's the big kiss-off. Emma got it and I didn't. I wish the floor would open up and I could fall through and never have to face anyone again.*

"Sam, you still there?" Billy asked.

"I'm here."

"So I called to offer you a spot as one of our backup singers," Billy finished.

"You did?" Sam gasped.

"Absolutely!" Billy said. "You blew us away! That's why we kept you on melody all the time—we pretty much needed to find two girls who blend with you."

"Oh, thank you, thank you, thank you!" Sam cried, jumping up and down with the phone.

"I guess that means you're accepting the job," Billy said, laughing.

"You got it!" Sam assured him.

"Great," Billy said. "Our first practice is tomorrow at four, out at our house. Is that cool for you?"

"I'll be there," Sam assured him.

"Cool," Billy said. "So I'll see you then."

"Hey, Billy, wait a sec," Sam said. "I know Emma's in but who's the third girl?"

"I guess I can tell you, since she already accepted," Billy said. "It's Diana De Witt."

Sam practically dropped the phone.

"Diana?" she repeated.

"Yeah," Billy said. "I think you, Emma, and Diana will look hot together, and you sound great. We're psyched!"

"Yeah, well, see you tomorrow," Sam said, and hung up the phone.

Sam slid down the wall until she hit the rug. The good news was she'd gotten the gig. The bad news was she was going to be spending lots and lots of time with Diana. *I've got to talk this over with Emma and Carrie*, Sam decided. *Emma!* She'd forgotten all about Emma waiting on the other line.

She pressed the phone button. "Hello?"

"Hi," Emma said. "I thought about hanging up, but I just had to wait and hear what happened. Was it Billy?"

"I got it!" Sam screamed.

"All right!" yelled Emma. "This is fabulous!"

"Think so?" Sam asked. "The third girl is Diana De Witt!"

Silence.

"Diana?" Emma finally said.

"Sort of takes the luster off, doesn't it," Sam lamented.

"Diana?" Emma repeated again.

"I see the very thought of her is making your IQ slump," Sam observed.

"Diana," Emma said for a third time. This time it was a statement.

"You got it," Sam said. "What fun this will be, huh?"

"Talk about taking the good with the bad," Emma groaned.

"No sugar, Sherlock," Sam intoned with disgust. "Just think. I get to be there when Diana steals Pres from me, if she hasn't accomplished it already."

"Maybe it won't be as bad as we think," Emma ventured.

"And maybe it'll be worse," Sam answered. "Maybe it'll be much, much worse."

ELEVEN

"Sam, we're out here!"

Sam heard Mr. Jacobs's voice cut through the early morning fog in her head as she walked downstairs into the Jacobses' kitchen the next morning.

He's calling me from the back deck. They must be having breakfast out there, she thought. *I hope now that Mr. Jacobs is a born-again stud muffin he isn't stupid enough to have let Tanya stay for breakfast.*

"Good morning," Sam said as she walked out onto the deck.

"Good morning yourself," Mr. Jacobs said. *No Tanya*, Sam thought. *That's a good sign.*

Mr. Jacobs gave Sam a half smile, seemingly reading her thoughts. "It's just us," he said, indicating the twins and taking a bite out of a buttered bagel.

"Hi, Sam," said Allie, looking up from her end of the bench.

"Morning," Sam replied, taking a sip of a freshly poured cup of coffee. "And you, too, Becky."

"Oh," said Becky. "Hi."

There is actually food on both of their plates, Sam thought with amazement. *Allie has a bagel with cream cheese in front of her, and it actually has bite marks on it! Okay, I'd better keep my mouth shut or they'll decide to fast for a month.*

Allie looked at Becky. "Should you tell her, or should I?"

"You tell her," Becky said. "I'm eating." She took a big forkful of cantaloupe as if to emphasis this fact.

"No, you," Allie said.

"No, you! Can't you see I'm chewing?" said Becky.

"Well, okay," Allie said.

Dan smiled at his daughters blithely, just happy that they weren't screaming at each other. Allie looked at Sam, a small grin playing over her lips. She took a sip of coffee in an effort to build the suspense. Finally, she spoke again.

"We got a gig," Allie said.

160

"Yeah, that's right, a real paying gig," Becky chimed in. "For money."

"That's great!" Sam forced herself to say. *Someone is actually going to pay real American dollars to hear Lord Whitehead and the Zit People do their thing?* she thought to herself. *They'd better get their paycheck before singing their first number!*

"It's like, major," said Allie, drinking some juice.

"Yeah, it's for Cleve Parker's birthday, and his father knows someone at Capitol Records," Allie said smugly.

Sam took another sip of coffee. "Who's Cleve Parker?" she asked.

Mr. Jacobs spoke up. "I know his dad, Arnold Parker. So how old is Cleve going to be?"

"Twelve," Becky admitted. "But he knows a lot of older kids."

"Hey, I'm sure you budding singers will be fantastic," Mr. Jacobs said. He looked proudly at his daughters, who both rolled their eyes in response.

"Dad, that is so bogus, " said Allie. "We're professionals now, get it?"

"Got it," Mr. Jacobs said, nodding solemnly.

Becky turned to Sam. "What about you, Miss Thing? Weren't the Flirts going to decide if you were good enough to sing backup for them?"

"Miss Thing?" Sam repeated.

"It's a rock 'n' roll expression," Becky explained with a toss of her head. "So what about it?"

"I'm in," Sam said with a grin.

"I knew that," Allie said, standing up to stretch. "The whole *island* knows that. Ian called this morning to tell me."

"So why didn't you tell me, then?" Becky demanded.

"Slipped my mind," Allie said with a shrug.

"Thanks," Becky snorted. "I bet I'm the only person alive who didn't already know."

"Well, I'm really proud of all three of my girls," Mr. Jacobs said fondly.

Sam attempted a pleasant smile. *Mr. Jacobs just called me one of his girls*, she thought. *Scary.*

"What's scary?" Allie asked Sam.

Oops. Must have said it out loud. "Getting your first gig is kind of scary, is what I meant," Sam explained.

"No, it's not," Allie said, sipping a glass of

orange juice. "Because when you're hot, you're hot."

"Right," Becky agreed. "And the Zit People are a lot hotter than the Flirts."

"And we're younger, too," Allie pointed out, "so we have a bigger future."

"Well, yes"—Sam nodded, sipping her coffee—"you certainly are younger, all right."

"So we'll see who gets the label deal first," said Allie.

Sam stopped drinking midsip. "Label deal?"

"That's right," Allie replied smugly. "It's called show *business*, Sam—it's not just how good you are, it's who you know."

"Yeah, and don't forget who Ian's father is!" Becky added. "Wilson Phillips got a deal, Julian Lennon got a deal, so why shouldn't Ian Templeton and the Zit People? Ian's father isn't even dead!"

Sam bit her lips to keep from laughing. "Well, that's a point, he certainly isn't dead."

"Anyway, we've gotta motor," Allie said, bending to kiss her father good-bye. "We've got band practice in half an hour."

"Hey, Sam, what are you guys going to

wear when you're on stage?" Becky asked as she got up from the table.

"We haven't even had our first practice yet," Sam replied, "so I don't have a clue."

"Well, whatever you wear, our outfits will be hotter," Becky said smugly, then she hurried out of the yard.

Before Sam could come up with a suitable retort, she heard the sound of a motorcycle pulling into the Jacobses' driveway. Sam's heart beat faster. *It's Pres, I just know it. And I don't really want to talk to him.*

Sam was right. Pres walked around the corner of the house into the Jacobses' backyard. Allie and Becky practically ran right into him.

"Hey, Pres," Allie said, "the Zit People got a gig!"

"Yeah," Becky chimed in, "and we're in the Zit People."

"That's great," Pres said, taking off his motorcycle helmet. He walked past them, straight to the table where Sam and Mr. Jacobs were still sitting.

"Mr. Jacobs, can I borrow Sam for an hour or so? I've got some band business I need to talk over with her." Pres spoke directly to Sam's employer, practically ignoring Sam.

"Sure, that'll be all right," he agreed. "Just have her back here by lunchtime."

"Excuse me," Sam said, her hands on her hips. "Did I just suddenly turn into a three-year-old or something? How about if I don't want to go with you?"

"That's why I didn't ask you," Pres answered.

"Well, too bad," Sam shot back. She folded her arms in front of her chest.

Pres sighed. "Okay, Sam. Will you come for a ride with me?"

"No," Sam answered.

"It's business," Pres added.

Sam narrowed her eyes. "Who cares?"

"Well, I sure hope you care," Pres drawled, "or you won't have this gig for very long."

"All right, I'll go," Sam finally said. "But just keep in mind that I don't work *for* you. I'm a member of the band, so you don't get to summon me whenever you feel like it. Got it?"

"Got it," Pres said sharply. He sounded about as angry as Sam did. He handed her a helmet.

Sam turned to Mr. Jacobs. "I'll be back by

noon," she promised, and walked silently with Pres toward his bike.

Pres and Sam climbed on, pulled out of the Jacobses' driveway, and set off on a short tour of the island. It was a glorious morning. The usual midmorning traffic heading to the beach area hadn't yet developed, and they sailed along Shore Road like a couple of birds, Sam's arms wrapped around Pres's muscled waist.

So what if holding him feels great, Sam thought. *That's just chemistry. That doesn't mean he isn't a two-timing jerk.*

Pres gunned the bike, and they sped up to about sixty miles an hour on the one long straightaway on Shore Road. The wind whipped past them. Sam turned her head to the right, and she could see the lobster boats out on the bay making their usual rounds.

Then Pres slowed the motorcycle, nearly to a crawl. He pulled it off the road at a picturesque spot overlooking the bay, cut the engine, and climbed off. Sam followed him to a pile of boulders by the water's edge. Much farther down the seawall, Sam saw a couple of kids fishing. She sat down next to Pres.

"Okay, let's hear this official band business," Sam said coldly.

Pres stared out at the ocean. "I know what's bugging you," Pres drawled, idly tossing small stones into the water.

"Oh, really?" Sam asked. "Then why don't you tell me?"

"It's Diana," Pres said, still tossing stones. "You're pissed off that she's paying so much attention to me, and you're pissed off that she's gonna be a backup singer."

"Well, aren't you the mental giant," Sam said. "And so perceptive! If your career as a musician doesn't pan out, maybe you should think about becoming a psychotherapist."

"Don't think so," he replied, finally looking at Sam, "because I haven't got the patience for stupid problems."

"Thank you so much for calling my problems stupid," Sam said sarcastically. "That really makes my day."

"What I mean is that you're too smart to get a hair up your butt because of Diana."

"This is more than 'a hair up my butt,' as you so eloquently put it," Sam shot back. "That girl is basically crawling all over you. You know she hates my guts, and then you

choose her to sing backup for your band—
next to me!"

"Hey, I didn't choose her!" Pres protested. "The Flirts are a band, remember?"

Sam harrumphed. "Well you sure didn't
say no," she shot back.

Pres was silent for a moment. When he
started to speak again, his tone was more
controlled. "Sam, our goal is to put together
the best band we can, and you know that."

Sam nodded.

"Because this isn't some kids' garage
group we've got here," Pres continued.
"We're pros. We want a contract, and we
want the brass ring. Sam, this is show
business, and business is business, Sam."

*That's the second time I've heard that this
morning,* Sam thought to herself. *I've
danced professionally. Why does he think I
don't know what it's all about?*

Sam nodded. "I know that, but I don't see
why—"

"Because she was one of the best people
we saw, that's why," Pres broke in. "And the
three of you will look great together—it
works." He let some sand sift through his
fingers.

"But isn't it important to have harmony on

stage?" Sam remonstrated. "Don't we all need to get along?"

Pres looked at her with his steely blue-gray eyes.

"Sam," Pres continued, "if we think that you and Diana and Emma aren't getting the job done, or we think that ya'll don't sound as good as we think you'll sound, I promise you we'll start looking for new backup singers in a New York minute."

"But—" Sam couldn't even finish her thought before Pres interrupted her.

"But nothing, Sam," Pres said. "It's show business. And if it was your band, you'd feel exactly the same way."

Sam sat on the rocks silent for a moment. *I know what he's talking about*, she thought to herself. *But that still doesn't justify Diana De Witt hanging all over him like moss on a tree!*

"You still haven't said anything about Diana doing everything she can to get into your pants," Sam said hotly.

"She ain't been in 'em yet, far as I know," Pres said simply. "Come on, Sam, it's rock and roll. It's a sexy business. You don't think that guys aren't going to be hitting on you at our gigs?"

"But it's not the same!" Sam protested.

"Why not?"

"Just because," Sam said, irritated that she couldn't think of a better answer. She sighed deeply, trying to gather her thoughts. "I guess . . . I guess it upsets me because we seemed to be getting closer," she finally said in a low voice. "I mean, I know we're not a couple or anything . . ."

"You didn't want to be one," Pres pointed out.

"Well, maybe I didn't," Sam agreed. "But . . . I don't know . . . you're the only one who really understands what I'm going through with my family, how stressful the whole thing is," Sam managed. "And it feels like I've lost my ally."

"Oh, girl, you haven't lost anything," Pres said gruffly. He put his hand over hers.

"But that's how it feels," Sam whispered. "I can understand about the band. But when I watch Diana flirting with you, it makes me crazy. If you had some enemy and he was all over me, wouldn't that hurt your feelings?"

"I can't say I'd like it," Pres admitted, "but I'd think he was a fool, not you."

"That's not how I see it," Sam said. "I

think if you care about me then my enemies should be your enemies."

"I think countries have gone to war over that kind of nonsense," Pres said, standing up. He helped Sam up from the sand, and put his arms around her. "Life is just too short for that," he murmured, looking into her eyes. "Besides, I have zero personal interest in Diana."

Sam backed out of his embrace. She wasn't convinced. "But you brought her to the clambake. You called her and told her she was a finalist! And you stopped calling me or seeing me at all!"

Pres laughed. "Is that what's bugging you? I thought for sure you'd get it. See, everyone knows you and I have something going. I wanted the auditions to be as professional as possible. So I thought we should just chill until it was all over."

"Well, how was I supposed to know that?" Sam demanded.

"Good point," Pres said, chagrined.

"And it still doesn't explain how you ended up at the clambake with Diana."

"Her car was in the shop. She called and asked me for a ride," he said with a shrug. "That's all it was."

"Why'd you call her to tell her she was a finalist?" Sam asked.

"I didn't," Pres replied. "She called me, and since the list was up and she asked, I told her she was on it."

"She lied to me!" Sam exclaimed. "She said you called her!"

"So why the hell didn't you just ask me?"

"Because . . . because . . . " Sam sputtered. "I'm going to kill her!"

Pres reached for Sam. "You're going to sing next to her, is what you're going to do. Can we make up now?"

Sam kissed Pres, but part of her was still angry. She would never let one of his enemies flirt with her, and she expected him to act the same way she would. *Yeah*, a voice inside her said, *except he's not you, and it's the music that's most important to him, so get a grip.*

All the way back on the motorcycle, Sam thought about it. But mulling their conversation over and over in her mind only made her more confused than ever.

When she walked back into the house, Sam could hear Mr. Jacobs on the phone.

"Yes, I'll take that number and make sure

she gets it—oh! I think she just walked through the door! Hold on—" Mr. Jacobs was saying into the phone. "It's for you," he said, "someone in Bangor."

Sam's heart leapt and a knot instantly formed in her stomach. *It's got to be someone from Family Finders*, she thought. *They're calling to tell me they got my papers.*

Sam took the phone. "Hello?"

"Hi, Sam, it's Audrey Birnbaum at the Family Finders Association. I have great news for you!"

Gee, she sounds awfully upbeat for someone who got a package of papers in the mail, Sam thought. "You got the papers I sent?" Sam asked.

"Yes, they've arrived," Audrey said.

"That's good," Sam said, still unsure why Audrey was so happy.

"That's not why I'm calling you, though," Audrey said. "Sometimes things just work out, which makes me so happy," she babbled.

"What things?" Sam asked, completely confused.

"I'm trying to tell you that we've contacted your birth mother," Audrey said. "She wants to meet you."

TWELVE

For a moment, Sam felt almost faint. She steadied herself against the wall with one hand.

"Wha . . . what did you say?" she finally managed to squeek out.

"I said we've contacted your birth mother, and she wants to meet you," Audrey repeated. "It happens this way sometimes. The West Coast office has had her application for quite some time, and we were able to match you up even without the extra information you sent."

"Where is she?" Sam asked.

"She's in Oakland, California," Audrey said. "That's right outside of San Francisco."

"Right," Sam said. Thoughts were milling through her head at a million miles an hour. And all she could say was "right."

"Anyway," Audrey continued, "we just called her and told her about you, and she'd like to call you, and then set up a meeting."

"This is just unbelievable," Sam said.

"It'll take you a while to digest it," Audrey said sympathetically. "So, can I tell Susan Briarly it's okay to call you, or would you rather call her?"

Sam pictured her birth mother calling during some chaotic moment at the Jacobses'. That would be awful. "I'll call her, if it's okay."

"Here's her number," Audrey said, and Sam jotted it down on the note pad by the phone.

"Let us know if we can be of any further help to you, Samantha," Audrey said. "It always makes me happy when we're able to connect families."

"Thank you," Sam said, staring at the phone number on the note pad. "I mean it," she added fervently before hanging up.

This is the phone number of your mother, Sam told herself. *Your real mother is only a phone call away.* A flash of guilt swept through her for thinking about this stranger as her "real" mother. Wasn't the woman who had raised her—her mom—her "real" mother?

Sam thought about the name she'd seen on her birth certificate. "Susan." Sam tried saying it out loud. "Hello, Susan. This is your daughter."

And then it occurred to Sam—she could call her right now. Right this very minute. She walked upstairs to be sure she had privacy, then paced in front of the phone, trying to get up the courage to actually use it.

Okay, you can do this, she said to herself. *This is what you've been waiting for.* With shaking fingers she dialed the California number.

"Hello?" answered a pleasant female voice. "Carson, the baby's knocking over the milk!" she called to someone.

"Hello," Sam said in a shaking voice that she tried to control. "Is Susan Briarly in?"

"Speaking," the woman said carefully.

She knows, Sam thought to herself. *I can hear it in her voice.*

"This is Samantha Bridges," Sam managed in a quiet voice.

"Yes," the woman breathed. "I know who you are."

Silence. *What am I supposed to do now?* Sam thought wildly. *What am I supposed to say?*

"I'm sorry," the woman finally said. "I'm . . . I'm overwhelmed. I've dreamed of this moment so many times . . ."

"Then you know who I am," Sam said. She had to be sure this wasn't all some bizarre fantasy.

"Oh, yes," the woman said softly. "You're my daughter."

For a moment Sam couldn't even seem to breathe. Tears came to her eyes and spilled down her cheeks. She had no idea what to say, where to begin.

"I . . . I guess you were looking for me, too," Sam finally said. "That's what the woman at Family Finders told me."

"Yes, and here you are," the woman said. "It doesn't seem real, does it?"

Sam could hear a baby start to cry in the background. The woman's baby. Her mother, Susan's, baby.

"Carson, could you burp the baby?" the woman queried. "She's got gas."

"Is this a bad time to be calling you?" Sam asked.

"No, no, please don't hang up!" the woman

said in a rush. "Let me just change phones, okay?"

Sam held on until the woman picked up again. The beating of her own heart seemed magnified in her ears.

"Okay, that's better," the woman said. "I'm upstairs and the family is downstairs."

"Do they know about me?" Sam asked.

"My husband does," the woman answered. "The kids don't."

Kids, Sam thought. *Kids that are my half brothers and sisters, who don't even know I exist.*

"The baby—Sarah—she's only ten months," Susan continued, "and I decided not to tell Adam about you unless I actually found you."

"How old is Adam?" Sam asked.

"Twenty-one," the woman answered. "He's a junior at U.C.L.A. studying film."

I have a twenty-one-year-old brother studying film at U.C.L.A., Sam repeated in her mind. *But how could that be? If I have an older brother, that means she was already married when she got pregnant with me, doesn't it?* She put her hand to her head. She felt flushed, as if she were getting the flu.

"I guess I don't really know what to say," Sam finally admitted.

"You must have tons of questions," Susan said. "I do, too. Oh, I can't believe I'm really finally talking to you!"

"Me, either," Sam admitted.

"I dream about you," Susan said softly. "I have for years. And I always hoped that one day you'd want to know me. . . ."

"I didn't even know I was adopted until a few months ago," Sam explained.

"Your parents didn't tell you?" Susan sounded shocked.

"No," Sam admitted. "They said they couldn't seem to find the right moment." As angry as that had made Sam, somehow admitting it to Susan made her feel she was being disloyal to her parents. She clutched the phone tighter. "They love me very much," she added.

"I'm glad," Susan said. "Could you . . . I'd love to hear about you," she said shyly.

"Well, I'm tall," Sam said nervously. "And I have red hair."

"Yes, go on," Susan urged her.

"I love to dance," Sam said. "I danced professionally at Disney World for a while."

"That's what you want to be, a dancer?" Susan asked.

"I think so. I just got into a band here, as a backup singer and dancer," Sam told Susan.

"That's great!"

"Yeah, I guess," Sam said. She felt like a fool, talking about these things, when what she really wanted to ask was the hard questions. In her mind she cried out: *How could I have an older brother? Who is my father? And most important of all, how could you give me up?* But somehow she couldn't bring herself to say these things to the voice on the phone. Instead she asked, "What do you do?"

"I edit children's books," Susan said. "Do you like to read?"

"Not really," Sam admitted.

There was another awkward silence.

"Look, I know you must have a million questions for me," Susan finally said. "It just seems impossible over the phone. Would it be okay if . . . I mean, I'd really like to come meet you."

"You want to come here?" Sam asked.

"The F.F.A. said you were working on some resort island off the coast of Maine."

"It's called Sunset Island," Sam said. "I'm an au pair."

"Would it be okay if I came there?" Susan asked Sam. "Meeting you would mean everything in the world to me."

"Yes, you can come," Sam whispered, gulping down her tears. "When?"

"Let's see, next Saturday?" Susan asked. "I'll get the earliest flight I can."

"All right," Sam agreed. She gave Susan her address and phone number at the Jacobses', then instructed her to fly to Portland and get the ferry to the island.

Finally they hung up. Sam couldn't move. She just sat there, feeling numb all over. The whole thing seemed like a dream.

She stared at the phone, as if Susan could somehow hear her thoughts through the instrument. *If meeting me would mean everything in the world to you,* Sam thought, *then how could you have ever given me up in the first place?* But until she could look Susan in the eye and ask her to her face, she had no answers. And her biggest question was whether she could bear to hear the answer.

"She's coming to the island?" Carrie asked Sam as they walked out by the pool in the

Parkers' backyard. It was early the next evening, and Carrie and Sam had helped bring over the Zits and their equipment so they could get set up before Cleve's birthday party.

It was funny, but Sam hadn't called either Carrie or Emma after she'd talked to her birth mother. The person who she thought would most understand was Pres, but when she called the Flirts' house, some girl said he wasn't around. After that she hadn't felt like telling anyone. It was a secret that she hugged to herself.

But now that she was actually with Carrie, she found herself blurting out the entire story and waiting eagerly for her reaction.

"Yeah," Sam confirmed, sitting on one of the longue chairs. She watched the Zit People setting their equipment up on the other side of the yard.

"Well, how do you feel about it?" Carrie asked. "Are you psyched?"

"I don't know," Sam confessed. "It's so . . . I don't even know how to explain what I feel. So much is running through my mind."

"I can imagine," Carrie sympathized.

"On the one hand," Sam mused, "I think

this is so cool—I mean, I probably look just like her, we probably have so much in common . . ."

"Maybe," Carrie said with a nod.

"But on the other hand, what if it's like meeting a complete stranger?"

"I guess you'll have to feel your way as you go," Carrie said.

Sam jumped up and paced nervously. "I feel like we'll just know each other," Sam said firmly, trying to talk herself into it. She whirled around to face Carrie. "Blood is thicker than water, right?"

"I don't know," Carrie answered honestly. "What about all that nature verses nurture stuff. I mean, you're bound to be more like the people who raised you than the woman who gave birth to you, aren't you?"

"Well, as we know I'm nothing like my parents," Sam pointed out, "which means I have to be like my birth mother!"

"Testing, one-two-three," Ian said into a live mike. "Turn the re-verb down on this, Garth," he told the sixteen-year-old boy who had just become their sound man.

"I hope Ian isn't embarrassed to death by this," Carrie said, looking over at Ian. "He's such a sensitive kid."

"I don't know how someone could have actually hired them, frankly," Sam said. "Has this kid Cleve or his parents ever actually heard the Zits play?"

"I don't think so," Carrie admitted. "I think Cleve is so impressed that Ian is Graham Perry's son that Ian talked him into this."

"Well, I'm ducking when the kids start throwing things," Sam announced.

"So, how do you like the threads?" Becky asked as she and Allie ran over and twirled in front of Sam and Carrie.

In the car the twins had been wearing shorts and T-shirts, but they'd carried what they'd called their "gig outfits" in a sports bag.

"Well, they're . . . interesting," Sam said, nodding.

"They're unique, all right," Carrie added.

The twins were wearing flesh-colored bodysuits, covered by see-through plastic raincoats with various objects hanging from them—including soup cans, hair spray cans, and cigarette butts.

"You probably don't even get it," Becky snorted with disgust, "so I'll explain it to you. We play industrial music, which is a

185

form of music that comes from living in an overindustrialized, seriously polluted society."

"Right," Allie said. "Right now we're dressed as walking pollution. It's a political statement."

"I see," Sam said gravely.

"Has it ever occurred to you two that you might be over the hill, musically speaking?" Becky asked.

"Don't bother talking to them, Becky," Allie said. "They clearly have no social awareness."

The twins flicked back their hair and walked away.

"I wouldn't believe it if I wasn't seeing it with my own eyes," Carrie declared.

"Since when are they politically aware?" Sam asked. "They don't even recycle!"

As Sam and Carrie continued talking, about thirty kids arrived for the party. They milled around outside by the pool, the boys trying to act like they weren't afraid of the girls, the girls trying to act like they could care less about the guys.

"Where did the band go?" Sam asked when she looked up from her conversation with Carrie.

"My guess is they're inside the house," Carrie said, "waiting to make an entrance."

"This is not going to be pretty," Sam sighed. "As nuts as the monsters make me, I feel badly for them already."

"I know what you mean," Carrie agreed.

"Hi, kids, I'm Cleve's dad," Mr. Parker said into the microphone to get everyone's attention. He was a chubby, balding man wearing too new jeans and a red golf shirt.

"Who cares?" one kid called from near the pool. A few other kids snickered. It was clearly so dweeby to have your father make announcements over a microphone at your birthday party.

"Welcome to Cleve's party," Mr. Parker continued good-naturedly.

"Yes, welcome!" his wife chirped from the sidelines.

"This is not exactly what I'd call warming up the crowd," Sam muttered to Carrie.

"It's my pleasure to introduce a great band," Cleve's father said, a cherubic smile plastered to his face. "Please welcome Graham Perry's son Ian Templeton and his band, Lord Whitehead and the Zit Men!"

"People!" one of the twins hissed from inside the house.

"I mean, Zit People!" Cleve's dad bellowed.

Ian and his band ran out of the house and took their places behind their appliances. The guys in the band were all dressed in black, and the twins really stood out in their colorful, multidimensional raincoats. *Actually*, Sam thought to herself, *the twins look kind of cute up there, in a bizarre sort of way*.

"Hello," Ian said into his mike with his new, affected British accent. "We'd like to open with our signature song, done the Zit People way." He turned and popped on the large tape deck that stood near him. The sounds of Richie Havens's "Motherless Child" filled the air.

Sam winced, waiting for the awful cacophony of sound about to assault her ears.

Only it didn't happen.

As Ian sang along with Richie Havens, the rest of the band beat rhythmically on their instruments. The twins swayed together in perfectly synchronized MTV backup singer fashion, as they chanted into the mikes.

No mother, no father, no sister, no brother . . .

And somehow, impossibly, amazingly, it worked. Lord Whitehead and the Zit People sounded good. In fact, Lord Whitehead and the Zit People sounded almost great!

"Have I lost my mind or is this good?" Sam whispered to Carrie.

"I like it, too," Carrie whispered back, "and so does the crowd."

The kids were all nodding along with the rhythms of the music, some joining in on the chorus.

"Sometimes I feel like a motherless child
Sometimes I feel like a motherless child
Sometimes I feel like a motherless child
Such a long, long, long way from
    home . . ."

When the song finished, the crowd roared. Allie and Becky hugged each other and started jumping up and down, they were so excited. And Sam thought if she could bottle and sell the happiness written all over Ian's face, she'd be a millionaire overnight.

"I'm so happy for him!" Carrie cried, clutching Sam's sleeve.

"I wouldn't have believed it if I hadn't seen it with my own eyes," Sam said.

"And heard it with your own ears," Carrie added.

"Thanks," Ian said into the microphone, starting to slip out of his accent. "Our next number is another rock classic." He clicked on the opening strains of "Gloria." This song was obviously not as far along, and the band sounded suspiciously like their old selves— awful.

"Well, at least they've got one number down," Carrie said philosophically.

"Listen, I never thought even *that* would happen!" Sam laughed.

"You never know, huh?" Carrie mused.

"That's for sure," Sam said. "Today Sunset Island, tomorrow the world!"

THIRTEEN

"I still think we should have worn the low-cut bra tops," Diana said as she, Sam, and Emma fixed their makeup back stage at the Play Café.

It was Saturday night, and after spending the week rehearsing over and over again, the Flirts were about to do their first gig with their new backup singers. The girls would only join the guys on the first set, because that was the only material they had had a chance to work on.

"Well, we voted, and you lost," Sam snapped at Diana as she sprayed her hair into a bigger mass of curls. Now that Sam and Diana were in the same band, Sam had no choice but to talk to her—which didn't mean that she enjoyed it.

The Flirts had told the girls they could choose their own onstage outfits, and the three of them had gone shopping together at the Cheap Boutique. Diana had favored all the low-cut stuff, since she had a much larger bust line than either Emma or Sam. Fortunately, her choices had all been voted down. Emma and Sam had chosen spaghetti-strapped mini-dresses of the same style but in three different electric colors—Emma in neon pink, Sam in neon green, and Diana in neon blue. The dresses were very short, but they skimmed rather than clung to their bodies. It was actually amazing that Emma and Sam had been able to agree, since their usual styles of dress were completely different. But somehow they had banded together against Diana.

And in fact, they seemed to band together against Diana all the time, which meant that Diana's cutting remarks were diffused. She had no ally when they were at band practice. And Pres, Sam was happy to find, was all business at rehearsal.

"What time is she arriving?" Emma asked Sam quietly, so that Diana wouldn't overhear and ask questions.

Sam knew the "she" Emma was referring

to was her birth mother, due to arrive on Sunset Island later that night. Sam had made plans to meet her at the Jacobses' at eleven o'clock.

"Eleven," Sam murmured, still trying to arrange her curls in the mirror. "God, my hair looks like a total wreck!" she yelled, and threw her comb across the room. She fell into a chair and buried her face in her hands. "I'm sorry," she whispered.

"My, my," Diana exclaimed, "and here I thought you were going to be so professional and all."

Emma shot Diana an evil look and went over to Sam.

"It's not the gig . . ." Sam said.

"I know," Emma commiserated. "If I were you I'd be a total wreck right now. I'd handle it a lot worse than you are."

Diana checked her lipstick one last time and turned to Emma. "If it's not the gig, what's she so upset about?"

Sam looked at Diana. "You are the last person on this earth I would ever confide in," Sam snapped, "so butt out."

"Well, *excusez-moi*," Diana intoned, turning back to the mirror. "And you're right, your hair does look awful," she added maliciously.

"Hey, ladies," Pres said, poking his head into their dressing room. "Ya'll look great."

"Thanks," Diana said throatily, walking over to Pres. "But don't you think showing a little more cleavage would have been hotter?"

"This is a great look," Pres said.

"Or tighter?" Diana asked. She held the sides of her dress taut across her full bust line and stared up at Pres.

"A little obvious," Pres said with a lazy grin. He moved past Diana and knelt beside Sam.

"Hey, sugar, how you doin'?" he asked Sam gently.

"Not so great," Sam admitted with a small smile.

Pres pushed some curls off of Sam's forehead. "Just try not to expect too much, okay?"

"You've told me that a thousand times in the past week," Sam sighed. "If she's anything other than a two-headed serial killer I'll be pleasantly surprised, okay?"

Pres laughed and kissed Sam softly on the lips. She couldn't help shooting Diana a smug look in the mirror—this was the first time Pres had paid special attention to her in a work situation. *Take that, Diana*, she said triumphantly in her mind.

"I'm gonna go finish tuning up," Pres said, standing up. "Ya'll kick some butt out there, okay?"

"So who is this two-headed serial killer who's coming to see you?" Diana asked after Pres loped out of the dressing room.

Emma turned to Diana with a haughty look. "It's a shame, really, that your own little life is so empty that you find yourself constantly listening in on other people's conversations."

Diana cursed at Emma under her breath, and Emma shared a smile with Sam. It was so much fun to get Diana's goat for a change.

"Hey, guys!" Carrie cried, sticking her head into the dressing room. "I just came by to say break both legs!"

"Show biz for good luck," Sam translated for Emma.

"Even I knew that," Emma said, laughing. "I can even say it in five languages!"

"Well, good luck in all five of 'em," Carrie said. She hugged Emma, then Sam, pointedly ignoring Diana. "I'll be out there videoing your big debut!" she called as she waved good-bye.

From off stage, Sam could hear the owner of the club, Ken Miner, introducing the Flirts. Her heart hammered in her chest, and she grabbed Emma's hand. For that moment all thoughts of her birth mother fled from her. All she could think about was trying to remember the harmonies and choreography to their opening song.

"I can't remember a thing!" Emma whispered frantically.

"It'll all come to you when you're up there," Sam assured her, even though she was going through the exact same mental blank as Emma.

"Please welcome the all-new Flirting With Danger!" Sam heard Ken cry.

The three girls whooshed past the backstage curtain and took their places on stage behind their microphones. Both Billy and Pres turned around to give them a reassuring grin, before breaking into the opening licks of "Maybe."

"Oooooo, oooooo," Sam sang behind Billy's first verse, swaying gently, touching her left foot to her right, then her right foot to her left as they had practiced. *Yeah, it's all coming to me!* Sam thought to herself with excitement. She looked over at Emma on her right. Emma had a smile on her face. Evidently it was all coming to her, too.

When the chorus came, the girls easily broke into their three-part harmonies, singing fully into the mikes. The song ended to thunderous applause.

"Way to go, Sam and Emma!" Sam heard Howie Lawrence call from near the front of the stage. She smiled at him as he put two fingers in his mouth and whistled through his teeth.

The next number "Do It to It!" was an up-tempo rocker with simple vocals and more difficult choreography. Now Sam felt more confident. She threw herself into the moves, dancing full out for all she was worth. She could feel the crowd loving it, and the more they loved it, the more of herself she put into it. *This is what I was born to do,* Sam thought to herself blissfully, as she spun around behind her microphone. *Only someday I want to be in my own group, with me front and center.*

This time the crowd really went wild, stomping and screaming. Emma and Sam hugged each other out of sheer exuberance.

The guys all looked happy, too—it certainly seemed as if the backup singer idea was working.

The rest of the set passed quickly. Sam missed one harmony line on "Paradise," a blues ballad Billy and Pres had cowritten, and once Emma missed a double turn into a hip roll on "Strange Sensation." Diana, annoyingly enough, was perfect. Still, when Sam went bounding off the stage, she knew that their first gig had been terrifically successful.

The crowd screamed for an encore, but the backups just shrugged at each other—they'd performed every number they'd had a chance to rehearse. Billy jumped back on stage by himself and picked up his acoustic guitar. The crowd hushed, and Billy sang the song he'd written for Carrie, looking directly out at her in the audience.

"This is the most romantic thing I've ever seen," Emma whispered to Sam.

After Billy's number, Sam ran back into their tiny dressing room.

"Whoa, that was outrageous!" she cried, throwing her arms around Emma.

"It's the most fun I've ever had!" Emma

agreed. "Except for that choreography I missed—"

"No one could tell," Sam assured her.

"I could tell," Diana said, carefully blotting the sweat on her face with a hand towel so as not to muss her makeup. She turned to Sam. "And you messed up a harmony line. It sounded horrible."

"Get a life, Diana," Sam snorted.

"Hey, Sam," a waitress called, sticking her head into the dressing room. "There's someone out here to see you."

"Must be a groupie." Sam laughed. "Is he cute?"

"He's a she," the waitress said, "like a mother type. She's waiting for you near the exit. Says her name is Susan."

Sam stood completely still, as if her feet had rooted to the floor. Susan. Her birth mother was here, right this very minute. She gave Emma a panicky look.

"I can't . . ." Sam began.

"Yes, you can," Emma said softly, gently touching Sam on the arm. "You can do anything."

Sam took a deep breath, then without a word she walked out of the dressing room and headed for the back of the club.

Instinctively Sam looked for a tall woman with red hair, someone flamboyant and fabulous-looking. But as she scanned the faces milling around, there was no one who looked even remotely like that.

"Samantha?" a quiet voice asked.

Sam looked down, and there was a small, plump woman with curly black hair going gray staring up at her.

"You're—?" Sam began, a puzzled look on her face.

"I'm Susan," the woman said in her quiet voice. She had tears in the corners of her eyes.

"But I thought you'd be . . ." Sam began. "You're early, aren't you?"

"I managed to get a different connecting flight that got me in early," Susan said. "Mr. Jacobs told me where to find you."

"Oh," Sam said. Now that the moment was actually here, she felt as if she couldn't speak at all. This small, plump, drab-looking woman was her mother? It just couldn't be true!

The jukebox started playing and loud music filled the air.

"Do you think we could go outside and talk?" Susan yelled over the music.

Sam nodded and they headed for the exit.

"There's a place we can talk around back," Sam suggested, and led the way to some boulders behind the club.

"You were wonderful up there," Susan said when she sat down.

"You saw me?" Sam asked in surprise.

"I got here right after your group was introduced," Susan said. "Someone pointed you out to me, but I would have known you anywhere."

"Because I described myself to you?" Sam said.

"Oh, no," Susan said softly. "Because you look exactly like your father."

Sam turned to Susan with a start. "My father?"

"He was . . . the handsomest man in the world," Susan said wistfully.

A hard lump formed in Sam's chest. "Is he dead?"

"I don't know where he is," Susan said. She stared out into the distance at the ocean. "I have so much to tell you, so much to explain. I don't know where to start."

"The beginning would be good," Sam suggested.

"I got married four years before I got

pregnant with you," Susan began, not looking at Sam. "My husband, Carson, and I really wanted to start a family right away, but I never got pregnant. Finally I went and had all these gruesome tests they give you to check fertility. The doctors finally told me there was zero chance I'd ever conceive. That was when we adopted Adam."

"He's adopted?" Sam asked with surprise.

Susan nodded. "We did it privately— someone knew someone—it didn't take very long. But I guess I was so busy being blissed out over being a mother that I ignored the fact that my marriage was falling apart. Carson is . . . I guess you could call him a very by-the-book kind of man. And me, well, I guess I've always been more of a dreamer."

"I'm like that, too," Sam said quietly.

Susan smiled at her quickly, then looked back out at the ocean again. "I think maybe I wasn't mature enough to handle marriage." Susan shrugged. "I had been a real hippie, free spirit and all that." She took a deep breath. "And I guess I wasn't really ready for motherhood, either—all the responsibility," she admitted. "Finally, everything just . . . fell apart. Carson and I were headed for divorce. I just had to get away from everything. So Carson stayed with Adam, and I took off for Israel."

Sam's head was spinning. "I thought you were so into being a mother," Sam said. "How could you leave your baby?"

"I knew it was temporary," Susan defended herself. "And Carson was—and is—a great father."

"Why Israel?" Sam asked.

"Well, because I'd never been there and I didn't know a soul there, which is just what I wanted," Susan answered. "And because I'm Jewish."

"You're *what?*" Sam asked.

"Jewish," Susan repeated. "Half, anyway. My mom was Jewish, my father was a Baptist. I wasn't raised much of anything."

"I'm *Jewish?*" Sam repeated.

"That's open for discussion," Susan said wryly.

"So . . . who's my father?" Sam asked.

"While I was in Israel, I met the most wonderful man. I was in Jerusalem, trying to find the Wailing Wall, and I asked a soldier for directions."

Sam snuck a look at Susan, who had a faraway look in her eyes.

"Who knows how or why things happen," Susan said. "I feel like it was fate. We fell in love."

"I guess you conveniently forgot about the husband and the baby back home," Sam said.

Susan was quiet for a moment. "I'm not telling you all this so you'll approve of me," she finally said, "because I know I made a lot of mistakes. I am trying to tell you the truth."

Sam bit her lower lip. In her heart, she thought she might be capable of doing something exactly like what Susan had done, so who was she to judge. "Go on," she finally said.

"I thought my marriage to Carson was over," Susan said, "and I'd spend the rest of my life with Michael. But two weeks later I got a call from Carson. Adam had meningitis. He was seriously ill."

"That's terrible," Sam murmured.

"I flew back home right away," Susan said. "Carson and I sat at Adam's bedside day after day, night after night, and I prayed for God to save my child. I know it's crazy, but I made a deal with God. I said, if you let my baby get well, I won't go back to Israel. Finally, slowly, Adam got better."

Susan allowed herself a small smile. "But something happened between Carson and me during those awful days," she continued. "I could see he loved Adam just as much as I did. Somehow, we became a family again. I kept my promise and I never saw Michael again."

"And you were pregnant with me?" Sam asked.

Susan nodded. "I guess the doctors were wrong," she said ruefully. "I had to tell Carson. He went crazy. He said he would never raise the child—that it would always remind him of my unfaithfulness."

"Then why didn't you just get rid of me?" Sam asked bitterly.

"I couldn't do that," Susan said. "I do believe in a woman's right to choose, but my choice was to have you, even if I knew I couldn't keep you."

"Why?" Sam whispered, tears in her eyes. "What was the point, if you weren't ever going to be my mother?"

"I just hoped . . ." Susan choked back a sob. "I always hoped that one day I could know you. But I always, always loved you."

"Did you ever tell Michael about me?" Sam asked.

"Never," Susan admitted. "I wrote him a good-bye letter. I never heard from him again."

"But he might have wanted me," Sam said, trying to hold back her tears.

"I think he would have," Susan agreed as she brushed the tears from her cheeks. "But I was afraid to have any contact with him, afraid of myself . . ." Susan took a ragged breath. "So I never told him. I'll feel sorry about that for my entire life."

Sam cried silently for a few minutes. The story was so sad. No. It wasn't just a story. It was her life.

"I look like him?" Sam finally asked, her voice muffled with tears.

Susan pulled a wallet out of her purse and took out a worn photo. "This is the only picture I have of Michael," she said. "I want you to have it."

By the light coming from the back of the club, Sam could make out the picture. She saw a tall man with red hair and a cocky smile on his face. She saw herself.

"I know I'm asking a lot," Susan said softly, "to want to be a part of your life now.

But . . . do you think there's any space for me?"

"You can't be my mother," Sam found herself saying. "I already have a mother."

"I know that," Susan agreed.

"But . . . I would like to know you better," Sam said. She gulped hard. "I just don't know if I can get beyond this feeling that you abandoned me. I don't know if I ever will."

Sam could see the tears making tracks down Susan's cheeks. "I understand," Susan whispered. "Maybe . . . we can just start out slowly. And see if we can at least become friends."

"Okay," Sam agreed.

"Okay," Susan said.

They both stared silently out at the ocean, until she felt Susan's hand lightly touch her hand. She opened her fingers, and let her mother hold her hand.

They both stared out into the night.

FOURTEEN

"Emma, bring more popcorn!" Sam yelled. "It's on the counter."

"You already polished off the first bowl by yourself," Pres pointed out.

"Hey, I'm a growing girl," Sam answered.

"You look full-grown to me," Pres said, leaning over to kiss Sam lightly on the lips.

Five days later the entire band was over at the Flirts' house to watch the video Carrie had made of the backup auditions. As Billy and Pres started to argue about the lyrics to a new song, Sam thought about everything that had happened.

Had it really been only a few days ago that she'd met her birth mother? Susan had stayed on Sunset Island for three days, then flown back to California. She'd promised to discuss Sam with both Carson and Adam, and she'd invited Sam to come visit them in California. Sam wasn't sure if she wanted to go—after all, Carson was the one who had rejected her completely, even before she was born. But something deep inside told her that eventually she'd make a trip there. Meanwhile, she and Susan planned to write and phone each other. They had so much to learn.

And then there was her mysterious father, an Israeli named Michael Blady whom she looked just like. Perhaps she'd try to find him—maybe she'd even go to Israel someday. Was he alive? Did he have a family now? Would he want to meet the grown daughter that he didn't even know existed?

"Here's the popcorn," Emma said, bringing Sam back to the moment. "It's got tons of butter on it, just the way you like it."

"Yum," Sam said, diving into the bowl.

Carrie made a face. "If that were me I might as well apply the butter directly to my hips," she sighed.

"Hey, you're perfect," Billy told her, tickling her ribs. "Don't rag on the woman I love."

"When's the video starting?" Diana asked

from her perch in an oversize chair. "I've got a date tonight."

"Right now," Pres said, pressing some buttons on the VCR control panel.

"It's showtime!" Sam yelled.

"It's not completely edited yet or anything," Carrie said, "so don't expect too much."

The TV screen came to life as the camera panned the Play Café at the first audition.

"There's me!" Emma cried. "I look scared to death!"

"That's because you were." Sam laughed. "Oh, there I am!" she hooted. "God, I'm cute!"

Pres threw a pillow at her, which she snatched off her face so she wouldn't miss a moment of the tape.

The camera came in close on Diana and Lorell. Now the general buzz of conversation gave way to Lorell's voice.

"You're a shoo-in, Diana," Lorell trilled. "Don't worry!"

"I don't know," Diana sighed. She looked over at Sam and Emma. "I think there's some tough competition."

"Just remember," Lorell said, a fake smile on her face, "never let 'em see you sweat."

"Oh, we're on to you now," Sam yelled across the room to Diana. "You were scared out of your gourd!"

"Hey, I'm human," Diana answered.

"You could have fooled me," Sam crowed.

"Shhhhh! I want to hear!" Billy yelled.

But no one was quiet for very long. They laughed and hooted their way through the tape, Sam the worst offender of all. She didn't even mind the parts where Carrie had caught *her* voicing her fears of not getting into the band. *Sure, it's easy to feel carefree now*, Sam thought, *since I actually got the gig*.

"Hey, you know, we really were the best ones," Diana said when the tape finished.

Sam stared at Diana, openmouthed. "Was that almost, sort of a compliment?"

"Don't let it go to your head," Diana said, flipping her legs over the side of the chair. "You're still blowing the harmony line on three tunes."

"I think your tape is great, Carrie," Emma said. "You really captured the tension of the whole process."

"It'll look even better after I edit it down more," Carrie said. "I loved making this— it's my first documentary!"

"Well, here's to many more," Billy said, raising his beer for a toast.

"Here's to the Flirts," Carrie said, lifting her glass of diet Coke.

"And to great friends," Pres added. He nuzzled close to Sam and whispered in her ear, "And I do mean great."

"Hey, hey, I've got a toast, too!" Sam cried, getting up on her knees.

"Well, let's hear it, girl!" Pres said.

"It's one I learned from my . . . from a friend recently," she said. "It's in Hebrew."

"Go for it," Emma urged her with a smile.

"L'Chaim!" Sam toasted them all, a huge grin spread across her face. At that moment it seemed to her that anything, everything was possible. "It means," she translated, "to life!"

"To life!" everyone yelled.

And they all toasted their futures, where everything was possible.

SUNSET ISLAND MAILBOX

Dear Cherie,

I was so excited to meet you when you signed my books last week. I just about died when I saw you were wearing red cowboy boots, just like the ones Sam wears! Is that where you got the idea for her boots? Which one of the girls is your favorite character? Who are you most like?

The Sunset Island *books are the best books I've ever read. I read them over and over. Could you publish them more often?*

> *Your fan,*
> *Andi Casnowsky*

Dear Andi,

It was great to meet you, too! You're right— I <u>did</u> get the idea for Sam to wear red cowboy boots because I wear mine so often. I really love all three girls on the island, but if I had to pick a favorite it would be Sam because she's the funniest. I suppose my own personality is a combination of all of them.

You'll be glad to know that there are more books coming soon, including <u>Sunset Paradise</u> at Christmastime, and in the spring, a new spin—off series called <u>Sunset After Dark.</u>

> All the best,
> Cherie

Dear Cherie,

I'm one of your biggest fans. I've read your whole sequence about Sunset Island with Carrie, Emma, and Sam. It's very well written. The whole series is interesting.

I'm fifteen and I have been interested in writing since I was in the third grade. Must you go to college to do this for a living? How do you get your ideas and who inspires you to go on?

Sincerely yours,
April Hayworth

Dear April,

I, too, got interested in writing when I was in grade school. Actually, my dad is a writer, so I was exposed to it early in life.

A good college writing program can be a tremendous help to your development as a writer. However, you learn to write by writing. I get ideas from my own life, from friends' lives, sometimes even from <u>The Oprah Winfrey Show</u>! The person who inspires me the most? My husband, Jeff.

Best of luck with your writing, April. Remember, always follow your dreams!

Cherie

Dear Cherie,

Hello! My name is Laura Chandler. My friends and I love your Sunset Island *books. They are really great. We're hoping you'll write more books continuing Emma, Sam, and Carrie's lives. Sometimes my friends and I talk about ideas for the characters, like what they might do in the future. Please keep writing your books because they are the best by far. We would really appreciate it. Thanks!*

Yours truly,
Laura C. Chandler

Dear Laura,

I wish I could have been there when you and your friends were talking about ideas for Sam, Carrie, and Emma! Why not write them down and send them to me? Who knows, you might just end up with one of your ideas in a future book.

Best,
Cherie

I love to hear your ideas and thoughts, so keep those cards and letters coming! Please include your name and address, and clearly state whether you want your letter printed. As always, if you'd prefer to have me answer you privately, just say so in your letter.

Cherie

Cherie Bennett
c/o General Licensing Company
24 West 25th Street
New York, NY 10010

P.S. If your letter is published, you'll receive a signed copy of the book it appears in!